Baby and the Panther

Victoria Sue

Cover Design by Vicki Brostenianc,

vickibrostenianc.com

Edited by Alyson Roy with Royal Editing Services

Formatting by Tammy Basile, Aspen Tree E.A.S.

Chapter One

Kai kissed Maddox's head and inhaled his clean baby smell. Maddox was so easy. He'd heard the other omegas share their own horror stories from difficult births to constant crying when he'd been back in North Carolina, and he had dreaded everything, but even Maddox's birth had been straightforward.

At least something is.

Alpha Shaun was kind. He'd seemed distracted by his pack so he hadn't really spent much time with Kai which was fine by him. He didn't set Kai's heart on fire, but he was *safe*. Maddox was protected, and that's what was important. Because Kai had learned a long time ago that being safe had to be his number one priority. He also seemed to be letting Kai recover from Maddox's birth. Kai knew that couldn't last forever as the whole point in him being here was to have babies, but he was grateful for the reprieve.

If he could just forget about a certain panther shifter, he had a chance at a happy life.

A deep sigh seemed to escape Kai's lungs. He supposed he would forget Marco eventually, or at least the constant pain in his chest would lessen to dull ache. He'd done the right thing moving away. He wasn't strong enough to see Marco every day and not be with him.

Kai's thoughts broke off as he heard shouting from outside and only had chance to glance up at the door to his room before it slammed open. Shaun's beta, Joe, accompanied by two wolf shifters he had never seen before, crowded into the small room. Maddox had jerked a little at the noise, but Kai automatically soothed him.

"You are required to come outside to the pack circle," Joe said stiffly.

Kai frowned. "I was just going to put Maddox—"

"That wasn't a request," one of the other wolves ground out. Alarm skittered up Kai's spine and his pulse jumped.

Kai clutched Maddox tighter and slipped into his sneakers. He followed them obediently out of the room. The pack circle was a large grassy area in front of the pack house that doubled as a meeting area before and after pack runs. Shaun was very traditional and disciplined. He required all his wolves to meet once a week and run together. He had a schedule for childcare but seeing as how there were only seven kids in total, Maddox being the youngest at six weeks and Tamzin the oldest at nine, it only took one person to watch them. Obviously for the past few weeks since he had come to live here, it had been Kai as he hadn't even been able to walk without waddling like an over-inflated elephant, and he certainly couldn't run. Not that as an omega he even had four legs to shift into, but he knew some omegas still joined in the fun, depending on the pack.

They passed the kitchen. Esme the cook had a pan on the stove, bubbling away, but she was nowhere in sight. He followed Joe to the door, both the other shifters walking menacingly behind him.

Kai tightened his hold a little, thankful Maddox was still asleep and walked outside. His gaze flew immediately to the pack circle and he forced his nerves deep down.

Standing about eight feet away was an older man. Maybe in his forties, but his age didn't lessen either the threat or the palpable danger he was giving off. Shifters didn't often put on a lot of weight as their animals controlled their metabolism, but this man was whipcord lean, his muscles stark against the reddish brown of his skin. A scar ran down the left side of his face and pinched his cheek tightly, drawing it in and lifting his top lip in a permanent sneer. Kai vaguely wondered what injury had been so bad he wasn't able to shift, but then it could have happened as a child. Then the thought of this shifter ever being a child seemed wrong somehow. He doubted if innocence had ever shone from the dark brown eyes that currently held nothing but cruelty.

Shaun—younger—his unmarked dark brown skin a startling contrast, also stood in the middle of the circle, stripped to his waist, and being held securely by two shifters Kai didn't recognize. Shaun's pack were all standing behind him at the edge of the circle. Kai made a move as if to join them, but the man in the circle saw him and grinned.

"Well, well, well, if it isn't the omega bitch, complete with whatever his sperm donor gave him."

Kai tried not to tremble, but his heart was trying to beat out of his chest. When the man gave a dismissive wave, Kai walked as quietly as he could and stood next to Esme. She met his eyes with a nervous look. He turned and gazed at the circle as two shifters—probably enforcers—walked Joe to the center.

The other alpha—because he obviously was an alpha—looked at Joe. "You have a choice. Get on your knees and ask for forgiveness and I will consider letting you live."

Joe's eyes narrowed. "Forgiveness for what?"

"Breathing," the alpha snapped out, and in a move so fast Joe didn't have a second to shift, the alpha blurred. Kai must have blinked because in the next second the alpha was back to standing on two legs, his ripped pants in tatters on the ground.

And Joe. Oh God, Joe. Blood pulsed from his neck as his hands tried to clutch his wound, but only for a second until they fell to his side. His blood loss had been so rapid, he hadn't had the chance to shift.

Kai turned his face away and breathed through his nose, trying to not to throw up. He looked toward the trees, debating escape. But as if one of the enforcers had read his mind, he stepped forward and gazed at Kai challeng-ingly, almost daring him to try and run. Kai turned back to the pack circle in defeat. The two wolves who had escorted Joe to the center of the pack circle carelessly dragged his lifeless body to the edge of the clearing.

"What do you want, Harker?" Shaun growled. Shaun knew him then.

Harker lifted one eyebrow as if he was considering his answer, then flung his arms wide. "Your land. Your pack." He grinned. "Your death." Two of the children and three she-wolves were already crying. Soft heart-breaking sounds they tried to smother.

"Let the pups go back inside. They don't need to see this," Shaun said.

"On the contrary," Harker responded. "It's never too early to be introduced to pack life. Pups need to learn what matters. That a dominant alpha always wins." He nodded to his enforcers and they let Shaun go.

"I'll even give you time to shift."

"Give me your word no other pack member dies, and I will forfeit." But Kai knew that wouldn't work. He'd seen the glee that blazed from the alpha's eyes, the type of madness, and the utter disregard for anything except how it could benefit him.

"Shift, or I kill you where you stand."

Shaun shifted. He was fast. *Just not fast enough.* Kai closed his eyes in despair. He heard the gasp from the pack and then deathly silence.

At the sound of another body being dragged away, he gulped and opened his eyes. People started moving. The pack was being herded into the group circle. Kai's heart, pumping so rapidly it almost felt like it was tripping over itself, threatened to stop altogether. And worse, Maddox finally registered the shouting around him and woke up. Being a baby he communicated the only way he knew how.

Crying.

Other pack members shot him sympathetic looks as Kai desperately tried to soothe him, but only milk would work, and he didn't have any out here. He didn't even have a pacifier, so Kai tried to use the tip of his finger which seemed to settle him a little.

Maddox quieted to a whimper, but Kai didn't think it would last for long. He rocked him, trying to calm his own racing heart in case the baby picked up on his fear. The next time he looked up, the circle was surrounded by even more wolves. Kai gaped. There were groups coming out of the trees, and he didn't know where from. Why would the alpha bring his pack here?

Harker raised his arms and everyone fell silent. "Friends, I promised you an auction."

Kai felt every drop of blood in him sink to his shoes. It was only the fact he was holding Maddox that kept him on his feet. These wolves weren't from the alpha's pack, they were gammas or enforcers coming from other places.

To bid for them.

He was going to be *sold*.

He had a moment to realize he wasn't breathing, but then a large male stepped forward. "I need enforcers."

The alpha nodded and seemed to peruse the pack. He lunged suddenly at Esme's son Chris who was about nineteen and a new gamma. Chris was too shocked to protest at being singled out and Esme gave a cry of distress.

They were given no choice. Kai felt a dig in his side and looked at Gerry, one of the older gammas. He was holding a phone. Kai took it shakily just before Gerry was dragged away. He quickly dropped it in his pocket before anyone noticed.

The auction went quickly. The wolves who got no bids—elders, usually —were manhandled to the back of the group. It was a nightmare. Children were separated from their families. Mated pairs were ripped apart uncaringly. One wolf who dared to object when his mate was dragged away was knocked unconscious and thrown aside. Harker singled out three young females, clearly intending to keep them.

Then it was Kai's turn.

He stood frozen, shushing Maddox or at least trying to, numb with fear but trying to convince himself that any pack would be better than belonging to this monster.

"Next bid's for a male omega. I prefer pussy myself, so I'm letting him go. You can see he's fertile."

And the bidding started.

Kai barely had a chance to see who had shouted a figure when the next bid was called out. His head spun, but through it all he kept a tight hold on Maddox and prayed. Not that he had a lot of hope. The types of shifters willing to do this didn't say much for their integrity. He just wanted Maddox safe and would do anything to make it so.

The bidding stopped and a man stepped forward. Older, unshaven. Kai tried not to breathe because the smell of liquor and body odor was so bad it made him want to gag. The man's hand snaked out and grabbed Kai's chin in a punishing grip. He tilted Kai's head left and right, then nodded. "He'll do. I need something to warm my bed."

Kai swallowed, completely sure he was going to vomit.

"But I don't want someone else's brat."

Kai had a second to process what he meant, then one of the enforcers ripped Maddox out of Kai's arms.

"No," he screamed and lunged for his baby. The backhand from the older man was enough to send him sprawling. Desperately Kai scrambled to his feet, but two enforcers just held him immobile with seeming little effort. "No," screamed Kai again as Maddox's wails grew louder, but Kai was simply dragged to the back of a van and thrown inside. He scrambled up, reaching for the phone in his pocket and called Emmett because it was the only number he could remember. He got out maybe ten words before the enforcers saw what he was doing. The next hit was so hard he was barely aware of hitting the floor.

Chapter Two

Marco was packing medical equipment away when his cell phone started dancing across the desk. He swiped at it, registered Ryker's name and answered it. "Hey."

"Meeting room, urgent." Ryker, his new alpha, clicked off and Marco grabbed his emergency bag and hustled. It was probably one of the kids. Although why he'd be summoned to the meeting room for that was anyone's guess.

Marco followed Chrissy into the room next to Ryker's office where the betas all met. Ryker, Chrissy, Fox, Red, and Sam, the new beta who had just transferred from a pack in Kansas were all in there. "Who's hurt?" Marco said looking around the room seeing no obvious injuries. Chrissy closed the door and Ryker looked up.

"Emmett got a panicked phone call from Kai about two hours ago. He told him his alpha has died in a challenge, Maddox has been taken from him, and Kai's been sold."

Marco froze, a chill sweeping over him so suddenly it took his breath.

"We can't get ahold of him. The number wasn't one we recognize and the phone's been turned off," Red added.

Marco looked directly at Ryker. "When do we go get him?"

Ryker nodded in acknowledgement. "We're waiting to find out from where. I'm not even going to attempt to stop you from being involved, but —" He glanced at his phone. "There's a call coming soon from whomever Zeke is arranging to cover you here. Pack what you need. Be ready in an hour."

"I'm ready now," Marco ground out. Ryker should have told him immediately. They had wasted two fucking hours.

"We don't know where he is," Ryker said. "Which is what we've been trying to find out. What we do know is that the challenge was won by a wolf named Karl Harker, and that Shaun Danvers and his beta are both dead. Harker's a mean SOB, but he's neither bi nor gay which is why Kai has been sold. We've managed to talk to a she-wolf called Esme who contacted another she-wolf from a neighboring pack. Esme's the cook, so she's been kept on. Her nineteen-year-old son wasn't as lucky and has been sold as an enforcer. Esme also says Maddox is still there as far as she knows, but all the kids have been separated from their omegas and an older she-wolf is with them in a separate room."

"The problem is," Chrissy added "Is that Karl Harker has at least fifty enforcers. There is no way we can get to Maddox easily."

"And?" Marco prompted because he knew from Chrissy's face there was something else.

"We can contact the Panthera," Ryker said.

"No," Marco bit out automatically

"She has access to the council, I don't," Ryker said. "We don't have to take the claw. To be honest I think the only way to do this is sneakily."

"Sneakily?" Red questioned.

"We haven't the wolves to go in all guns blazing and create a pack war. We find out where Kai is first. Esme has a phone hidden and I've promised her when we get Maddox we'll also take her."

Chrissy snorted. "And the rest."

"Her son. I promised that as well."

"And as far as we know they're in different packs," Chrissy pointed out.

Ryker shrugged. "We rescue shifters. This is what we do."

Marco turned on his heel and went to pack. *The Panthera?* Panther shifters were completely different than every other shifter group he knew. The alpha equivalent of the panther pack—or clan—was the Panthera, the head female, and the title passed down the female side. He knew they considered Emmett's grandma—the Panthera for her own clan—different, but he would never forget his own. He forced the sick images down of the last time he'd seem his. The night he'd nearly died because he'd committed the ultimate betrayal of falling in love with a human. Except it hadn't just been the claw—the Panthera's enforcers—that had made him suffer after being beaten almost to death as an act of betrayal. It had been her.

"He's a reporter!" The Panthera screamed in his face and had waved the article at him. "Do you know what this will do to me?"

He had known. Still stunned with being used by the man he was ready to risk his life for, it had taken him a few dangerous seconds before he'd worked out the real reason the Panthera was so furious. She'd already taken care of the "problem." Money, threats and an "accident" had worked as it usually did, but the shifter council had been informed. Any threat to discovery of shifters by the human world merited swift and usually very costly punishment. The Panthera was the clan leader of the entire west coast. The clans under her contributed financially to her already astonishing wealth, and it was likely she was going to be made head of the shifter council.

Or it had been. That was what she had lost. And why her claw had beaten him over and over for three days until he was too broken to shift anymore. He lay in a pool of his own blood and piss as she bent over him, lifting his head by his hair, spitting as vitriol poured from her mouth. She asked him over and over if he understood what he had done, and finally he had whispered, "Yes, Panthera," before she slammed his head back down so hard he lost consciousness. But what he actually should have said was, "Yes, Mother."

Marco blinked away the memories and set his jaw. Guilt was clawing at his carefully constructed defenses. *It's my fault.* Kai had left because Marco wouldn't step up. He knew Kai was his true mate, *of course I do.* But knowing what had happened to James meant he couldn't ever risk her finding out about Kai. Because while mating humans was strictly forbidden, inter-species mating was considered a worse crime.

So, to protect Kai he had refused to acknowledge they were mates, and the stubborn, completely gorgeous man had left because of it. He'd thought Kai would at least stay in the area.

He'd been wrong. And in trying to save Kai's life, he might be responsible for ending it. Because Kai wouldn't survive without Maddox.

Maddox. In his mind's eye he could almost see him. He'd bet he had the same hazel eyes and light olive skin as his omega. Marco shoved spare clothes in a backpack and made sure his medical kit was up to date—not that he ever risked that it wasn't, but he wanted to be extra careful.

It took him no more than twenty minutes, then he headed for the kitchen. He wanted some snacks to take with him. Something he could give Kai in case he needed it.

Dinah met him at the door, tears in her eyes. She nodded to a bag on the side. "Protein bars and powdered milk." Marco squeezed her gently in thanks. He hadn't thought about Maddox needing food. Some medic he was. "I also packed some spare clothes and diapers in case you need to leave in a hurry."

Chrissy walked in a few moments later. "Ryker's saying goodbye to Emmett." Marco caught the shared look. Emmett had just given birth for fuck's sake and now Ryker was having to go to Mississippi. Dinah hugged Chrissy.

"I won't leave him."

"Zeke's also staying here until we get back."

Ryker strode in moments later. "Marco, Red, Chrissy. We can all fit in my truck and I can rent another one down there. I'm leaving Fox and Sam here so the pack house has protection. Mills River only knows that we are leaving on a rescue but no details. They will help with security."

Red walked into the kitchen. "Truck's loaded."

"We'd better get going then. The trip takes about seven hours."

Red scoffed. "Not if Chrissy drives."

. . .

Marco stared through the window as the highway stretched endlessly into the dark night. He couldn't sleep. He'd half-heartedly offered to drive but had been glad no one seemed inclined to take him up on it.

Ryker's cell phone rang and he answered it immediately. He listened for a moment, then glanced up at the next sign. "Come off here," he directed to Red, who was currently driving, then continued to listen. Marco pushed down his impatience. They weren't even at Birmingham yet, and now they were headed toward Talladega, not to Mississippi.

"Thanks, Zeke." Ryker clicked off. "Jarvis Samson is the alpha of a small pack. He hasn't got any land, but he seems to own some storage yards in and around Talladega that are a front for a fentanyl distribution business. He's allowed humans to rent storage space from him. One yard on the outskirts of Jonesville is where his pack house, if you can call it that, is." Ryker stared at Marco. "You're the only one of us who can pose as human. If he has Kai, he'll be at the pack house."

"Or crack house," Chrissy muttered. Marco curled his hands into fists.

"Zeke's setting you up a backstory. You want somewhere quiet to store exotic imports," Ryker continued.

"Exotic—" Marco's eyes widened. "You mean animals." It was a huge illegal business in the US.

"You are one of the largest exporters of Asian leopard cats. You're expecting a shipment of kittens, but you've just lost an import area due to a raid. You're angry because you don't like to involve other people, but at $8,000 per kitten you need somewhere fast."

"How does Zeke know all this?" Marco said in astonishment.

Red chuckled. "My mama would say 'a man isn't wise because of *what* he knows but *who* he knows.'"

"Plus, Samson has just lost a lucrative contact. A competitor forcefully took a whole area of distribution from him and he's hurting. The temptation to get out of the drug business, or at least to diversify, will be huge, so he'll want to impress you."

"How are we going to get him out?"

11

Ryker blew out a breath. "Apparently Samson puts on entertainment for his friends. Drugs, girls."

Marco winced.

"But he's just been advised you're gay."

The silence in the car was explosive. Marco felt sick. "He's likely to offer Kai?"

"We don't know for certain, but it's a working theory. Once you locate Kai, we will arrange an escape. But we need you out of there first, because as soon as we have Kai we have to go get Maddox. We can't have Samson guess anything and warn Harker. If you can't contact us, we will just come at a prearranged time."

"You have to be convincing. Kai's not stupid. He'll play along," Chrissy said.

Play along with what though? That he wanted Kai with every breath in his body? That he ached to hold the man close? See his gorgeous smile and know he had put it there? That he had made the biggest mistake of his life letting him leave?

That wouldn't take any convincing at all.

Chapter Three

here am I?

Kai woke lying on a bed. It wasn't a huge bed and he was alone in the small room. For a second, he stared at the chipped paint and the stain in the corner of what used to be a white ceiling. His fingers curled as memory flooded in. He was used to waking with the comfort of Maddox. His smell, even his crying. Where was he? Was he safe? *Is he crying for me?*

His heart hurt even more than his head, and he put up a hand to touch his throbbing cheek. He sat up gingerly and saw the glass of water on the old nightstand next to the bed. He was thirsty and reached for it cautiously. He might be a non-shifting wolf, but his sense of smell was usually still pretty accurate. Plus, if someone was going to poison him, why bring him here. Then he remembered exactly who had brought him here and he swallowed the nausea down, taking a settling sip of the tepid water.

He'd had a chance to call Emmett, but he had no idea where he was now. Would they come for him? Would they even be able to find him? Would they even bother when it had been his idiotic decision to leave?

He took in the rest of the room and could hear the sound of traffic from outside. There was a small window. He stood, waited until his head stopped spinning, and walked over to it. He scrunched up his nose and peered out at what looked like some sort of industrial yard. Two beat up cars. Another one on blocks. And in the distance he could see garages, storage units. A town. He'd never lived in a pack that was in a built-up area. He glanced to the corner, saw a door and hoped it was a bathroom. It was, even if it wasn't very clean, but he quickly used it and washed his hands. Not that he had anything to dry them with. He also longed for a shower as he was still dressed in the clothes he'd had on yesterday.

Had it even been yesterday? He could easily have been given something to make him sleep longer. The water threatened to make a reappearance. There were another two doors. He assumed the one by the side of the bed was for the room, and the one by the bathroom...he tried it and yes, a small closet. Mostly empty with what looked like— He picked up a small purple shirt. It would fit him...just. He saw the tight ass jeans, the tiny shorts and the beaded tank tops and shivered.

He'd gotten the distinct impression that his new role didn't require clothes. He had a minute of gut-wrenching loneliness, but then he took a breath. He would wear anything if it helped him escape and get to Maddox. *I would do anything.* He just had to work out where he was first, and then how to get free.

He'd told Emmett that his dad had died in a hunting accident, but he'd lied. He hadn't wanted to admit to a perfect stranger his dad had been so disgusted with him he'd thrown him away.

He'd been seven the first time he'd upset his dad. He'd been helping his mom by standing on a chair in the kitchen wearing his sister's new skirt so she could pin up the hem. He wasn't into dresses, but he didn't mind helping his mom, who had promised cookies as a reward. When his dad had come in with their alpha, everyone had gone really quiet.

Their alpha had turned to his dad who was visibly squirming and asked if Kai had shifted yet. His dad had responded that he was only seven, but the alpha just shook his head. Mom had apologized and explained what they were doing. Kai hadn't understood why everyone was so mad. He got that it wasn't what boys did. He'd had that rammed into him by his elder brother. But the skirt wasn't his, it was a surprise for Ellie.

14

It wasn't like he was going to actually wear it. And his mom's cookies were fabulous.

But his dad had changed. Instead of being allowed to curl up with his books, he'd had to go outside to "play" and he hated it. There were all sorts of nasties. Bugs, snakes. *Yuck.* Garth had even dropped a tiny lizard down his shirt once and he'd screamed until his mom had come and got him. And his dad started criticizing everything. He wasn't supposed to like the pack school or to be good at art. He was supposed to skip lessons like Garth and constantly get into scrapes or into trouble. So, he had just kept his head down and waited to grow up.

Then, when his younger sister—fourteen months his junior—had shifted at eleven, everyone was so pleased and proud. The next day the pack's alpha had died in a hunting accident and the alpha's uncle had taken over and everything had changed once more. All the wolves who had never shifted but were over eight had been taken to the pack circle and told they were going to run and that the gammas were going to chase them. Some of the older wolves had protested, but the new alpha had just said it was a good way of bringing on a first shift. There had been six of them and it had been one of the worst nights of his life. They'd run them into the ground. Exhausted, crying, terrified he'd finally been cornered by two of the shifted wolves and he'd expected to die. Then one of the wolves had shifted. Kai had then cried, but in relief, because it had been his dad.

His dad who said he was ashamed of Kai. That he was no son of his. Kai had been marched back to the pack house and moved into a separate room with three of the other children. One had shifted and was back with his family, and one had fallen, ripped open his leg and bled to death because he couldn't shift.

Gone were the books and cookies. He didn't even get to see his mom. He saw Garth and his dad a few times as all the males ate together and as part of his new omega duties his was expected to wait on them. Garth hadn't dared look at him or acknowledge him, but by this time Kai knew better than to try.

The women were housed separately, even the mated females were no longer allowed to walk around without their mate or a gamma escort.

Then, the morning of his sixteenth birthday, he'd been dragged out of bed while it was still dark and told he'd been sold. That had been the first time. The second had been twenty months later and that time he had been thrown out when his alpha had gotten a wife. He never saw any of his family again.

Shaking off the memories, Kai tried the other door, not surprised it was locked, and sat back down on the bed. He was just contemplating what he was going to do when he heard the door unlock. He scooted quickly up to the wall, knees to his chest. He didn't recognize the thug who came in first or the older man who followed pushing a cart. He smelled food, so at least that was good.

"Where am I?"

The older man sighed tiredly. "Your new alpha is Jarvis Samson and this is his pack house."

"Where?"

Kai shrank back as the thug raised his hand as if to backhand him, but the older man caught it. "Alpha's instructions were to hide his injuries. I can't do that if you inflict new ones."

The gamma swore, but he folded his arms and went to stand by the door. Kai took it to mean he wasn't allowed to ask questions. The older man uncovered a plate with two sandwiches. They were mostly bread, and by the smell peanut butter, but he was starving. The old man saw Kai's hesitation. "It's safe. He wants you for tonight, so he isn't going to poison you."

Kai swallowed. "Tonight?" Suddenly he wasn't so hungry.

"He's entertaining a guest. He wants you there." *To fuck him.* Kai didn't need a diagram. He knew what to expect. It wouldn't be the first time he had been entertainment. He eyed the sandwich. He couldn't escape if he wasn't strong, so he took a bite.

"Call me Charles."

Kai nodded warily. He'd been okay so far. Not exactly friendly, but he hadn't tried to hurt him. He finished the sandwiches and let Charles shave him. Apparently he wasn't allowed to even wash himself, let alone be trusted with a razor, but Charles was impersonal and brisk. After a while the gamma even left and Kai relaxed a little. Charles made it clear he wasn't going to answer any of Kai's questions. He simply told him not to fight it as everything would go easier on him. The final humiliation was the enema.

Kai balked until Charles let him see to it himself. When he finally let himself out of the bathroom after getting cleaned up, Alpha Samson was there and Charles stood gazing at the floor. Kai immediately noticed the red mark on Charles's face, and for the first time saw how thin he was.

Samson's eyes gleamed as Kai walked into the room, and he yanked the towel from his waist. A second later Samson's hand gripped the back of his neck so Kai couldn't move and his other hand fondled Kai's balls. Kai stood stock still willing himself not to react and it was mostly the revulsion at Samson's touch that kept him flaccid.

Samson let him go with a snort of disgust and turned to Charles. "You'll have to give him something. I need him begging for it."

A chill snaked down Kai's spine replacing the disgust. "Give me something?" He'd taken something before to bring on his heats. The first one had been painful and embarrassing. At sixteen he hadn't understood what was happening to his body and why he had gone from shy to needy in the space of a couple of hours. It had been confusing and one of the most humiliating nights of his life. He was lucky that along with the tonic to bring on his heat, they'd also used condoms because humans had only wanted to protect themselves from disease. His last alpha had been better, gentler, but after so much cruelty and indifference, Kai had mixed up someone being nice to him with a declaration of love and he'd fallen hard. Kai had still needed to take something. But he had believed the bastard when he'd said it was what happened to all omegas. Not that it was because they weren't mates. In a lot of ways getting drugged that time had been worse.

"No."

Kai hadn't realized he was going to say it until he heard the word from his own lips. "No, I'm not taking anything." He looked defiantly at Samson and saw him fist his hands, recalling that Samson didn't want him to have injuries before tonight. Not that he was under any illusion he might not get them later. Samson might be a slob, but he was easily twice the size of Kai and could no doubt do some damage.

Samson stepped up and grabbed Kai's chin in a punishing grip. "You will do as you're told. There are plenty of things I can do that won't leave bruises." He yanked his hand away and nodded to the enforcer. "Hold him down."

The enforcer's eyes gleamed as he stepped forward. Charles pressed his lips together as if to stop himself from making a sound. Kai swallowed and backed up. "I said no. I didn't say I didn't understand I was going to get fucked, just that I don't want to be drugged." If he was going to be raped, he wanted to fucking look the bastard in the eyes, not be out of his mind with lust.

Samson ignored him. The enforcer didn't waste a second, and within a moment Kai was flat on the bed completely unable to move. He clamped his lips shut when Samson brought a bottle out from his pocket. He met Kai's eyes and Kai glared defiantly. Samson snarled at Charles and Charles closed his eyes but held Kai's head still. Samson simply leaned over and pinched Kai's nose.

He struggled uselessly and was forced to open his mouth to take a breath. Samson was quick. He forced the liquid down Kai's throat, then held his chin closed and kept his grip on Kai's nose until he swallowed. He desperately tried for another breath, but he was forced to swallow another two times.

"Alpha," Charles said desperately. "It might be too much."

But Samson just laughed and nodded for the enforcer to let him go. "Tie his hands so he doesn't get any ideas about making himself throw up."

Kai sent such a look of betrayal Charles's way the older man visibly flinched, but Samson either didn't see or didn't care. Kai closed his eyes as Charles quickly changed him. He didn't care what he wore. As far as he was concerned the only thing keeping him alive at this point was his determination to get back to Maddox.

Less than five minutes later, he knew he was in trouble. His limbs started to feel heavy, and his blinking slowed to the point he had to push his eyes open. He opened his eyes wide and looked almost dispassionately at the enforcer who was grinning down at him.

"Shame he's not mine," the man said. "But no one said I can't have some fun." He trailed light fingers down Kai's bare chest and Kai had to struggle to keep his gasp contained. His nipples pebbled involuntarily even though he hated the touch.

"Alpha ordered him to be kept under," the older man said. Kai's eyes tried to focus. What was the man's name? "You know if he comes it will lessen the effectiveness." The enforcer made a disgusted sound but stepped back.

Kai was aware of people talking. At one point he was helped up and directed to another room. He didn't walk, he floated. If the man hadn't kept ahold of him he honestly thought he might fly away. Every inch of his body pulsed and his skin felt alive. He drifted into the other room, quite liking that the talking seemed to stop when he entered. It made him feel almost powerful and he liked the eyes on him. Another man tugged him closer. Was this the alpha? He didn't like him, but objections burst like bubbles on his lips before he could form any. Why couldn't he remember his name? Not that it really mattered. Nothing seemed to matter. Not when he was all relaxed and floaty.

"Kai, we have a guest. I'm sure you want to make him feel comfortable." The alpha turned him too quickly and he stumbled. A giggle burst from his chest as he tried to focus on the newcomer.

Deep gray eyes stared back at him. Dependable, yet sexy. Faint recognition stirred in him, but his thoughts were too jumbled to grasp. He was powerful. The man stood as Kai took a step towards him. He clasped Kai's hands and Kai was certain he would have fallen if the man hadn't taken hold. Kai gazed up and down his body. Lean. Strong. The type that Kai liked, or that he liked to have his hands on. Or better still have the man touch him. A shiver of something delicious skittered over his skin and Kai felt himself harden.

The man was still holding his hands, his thumb stroked gently over the skin between Kai's thumb and forefinger. Kai looked down in puzzlement. How was having his hands rubbed such a turn on? "You smell wonderful."

The man's smile faltered a little, but his hands tightened and Kai took another step closer, stumbling again. His legs were like jelly.

The alpha smiled, seeming pleased. "Why don't you get comfortable while we get to know each other, Santoz?"

"Santoz?" That wasn't right, not that Kai knew why he thought that.

"Call me Marco."

The other man made a pleased sound, but Marco wasn't looking at him. His gaze never left Kai. Marco was a good name. That fit. Marco tugged Kai to sit down, but next to him wasn't close enough and Kai half-sat/half-fell onto his lap. Kai felt Marco try and pull away a little, but he didn't give him a chance as he curled over him. Kai inhaled, pressing his nose against Marco's neatly trimmed beard and rubbing his cheek along it. Marco's hand fell to Kai's leg and he wriggled a little as a flare of heat coursed through him at the touch. Kai moaned breathlessly and tried to inch closer. The alpha laughed, but Marco just tightened his hold and Kai shivered letting the conversation drift over him. He could hear the thudding of his heart and he slid his fingers in between the buttons of Marco's shirt, desperate to feel his skin. Marco's hand caught Kai's wrist, but he didn't falter in their conversation.

Kai didn't care about *Hyacinth Macaw's* whatever they were or the immediate storage problem the alpha thought he could help Marco with. All he cared about was getting as close to as much of Marco's bare skin as possible.

Kai's lips pressed against Marco's neck and he licked him. Marco took his hands in his and pressed him even closer as Kai tried to grind himself against Marco. They were still talking, but Kai wanted all of Marco's attention on him.

"I think we may be able to come to some sort of arrangement," Marco said at last. "I would need some assurances of course. I cannot afford to be mixed up with someone who draws attention to themselves."

The alpha nodded eagerly. "Why don't you relax while I arrange some practicalities?" Kai knew he meant with him and he hummed his approval.

Marco inclined his head. "And I assume you have a private room we can relax in?"

"Of-of course," the alpha rushed out. Another moment and he was back. Kai tried to stand rather unsuccessfully. Marco seemed to make an impatient noise and clamped his arm around Kai to keep him upright. A shiver ran down Kai's spine and he leaned in. Marco might as well have been carrying Kai because he gave him all his weight.

Kai barely glanced at the room they were shown. He knew it was large, but he didn't care because he wanted nothing more than to focus on Marco and getting them both undressed. Not that Kai had a lot of clothes on, but Marco was in a suit.

Kai tried to coordinate his fingers enough to undo Marco's shirt buttons. Marco sighed and caught his hands to stop them. Kai blinked slowly, a little puzzlement crossing his features. Marco just hugged Kai close, and while Kai loved the attention, that wasn't what he needed right then. Why wouldn't he touch him? Didn't he like him? For some reason that thought hurt. "What's wrong?"

Chapter Four

hat's wrong?

W Marco gazed at Kai. What was *right* with this scenario. Kai was as high as a kite. He'd obviously been given something. The trouble was it could range from human Rohypnol or GHB to a mixture of those with animal tranquilizers for shifters that made the whole concoction very dangerous.

Omegas were just as susceptible as humans to the effects, but their shifter physiology also meant they blew through human drugs a little too quickly. The effects were similar, but it didn't cause complete memory loss after and they were usually semi-aware. He'd deliberately taken his time with Samson to give Kai a chance to recover some. It had made zero difference which meant the chance of him being given the newest omega mix version was off the charts. It's third ingredient was similar to Viagra given to humans. The trouble was Marco had recently seen omegas die from the mix. Humans certainly wouldn't survive such a cocktail and it often brought on seizures and death.

The only sure-fire way of bringing an omega down from the false high was an orgasm. More than one. It was the fastest way to steady their heart rate and what Marco knew would be spiked blood pressure. The bastards who used the drugs enjoyed how long they could edge an omega without bringing them relief. The shifter could orgasm all night and by giving the omega no relief it would keep them high and desperate. It was disgusting, but it put Marco in an impossible situation. He was supposed to get Kai out. The diversion had been arranged for midnight, which meant they had only forty minutes to go, but Kai could barely walk. There was no way to contact the others. Marco had had to surrender his phone as he entered which didn't surprise him. Chrissy had given him a burner phone—a high class one to fit his persona—because they knew it was likely. So, he needed Kai aware, mobile, and capable of being silent. Kai was none of those things, he moaned and writhed against his leg looking for some relief.

Marco had no intention of fucking Kai. In his current state it would be rape pure and simple, but wasn't touch without Kai's permission the same thing? Even if it would save his life? Marco brushed a hair from Kai's sweat-slicked skin as Kai struggled to open his eyes. Both his pupils were huge and he whimpered.

If the drug followed its normal course, the muscle cramps would be starting soon. The idiot had given him way too much. A knock at the door surprised Marco and he quickly bent and took Kai's lips in case it was Samson. The sound of a whispered apology and two bottles of water being put down made him look up. The older man who had brought Kai into the meeting room was looking at Kai in fear mixed with a healthy dose of distress.

"What's he on?" Marco growled, risking a lot but he had to know.

"Just something to make it easier," Charles whispered.

"For whom?" Marco bit out. "He can hardly take part and I like my boys to at least know who's fucking them."

He lurched upright and Kai shivered and moaned again. "I'm going to have to wait until he comes down a little," Marco added irritably laying it on a little thicker. The immediate look of alarm told Marco all he needed to know. That Kai couldn't be "left alone." The longer this went on the higher the risk of seizure or stroke.

"I—" Charles twisted his hands uselessly and shot a fearful glance at the door. Marco wanted to ask him for help, but the chance he was more frightened of Samson was pretty fucking likely, and he might just go to him.

"Leave me," Marco ordered, and Charles practically fell over himself in his hurry to get to the door, but then he stopped and met Marco's gaze.

"He needs to get off. It's dangerous if he doesn't. And if you tell the alpha he'll kill me."

Marco was stunned as he watched the older man close the door behind him. Whatever he was petrified of, he had risked a lot by trusting Marco. He glanced at his watch. Twenty-five minutes to go. If he was going to do something it had to be now. "Kai? Kai, sweetheart?"

But Kai didn't answer. He couldn't even open his eyes, just moaned, shivered and twisted as he tried to reach Marco, his hands shaking badly as he clasped Marco's shirt. Kai would have to just hate him afterwards.

An ache blossomed in Marco's chest. Who was he kidding? Kai already hated him. He quickly stripped the sweat soaked shorts off Kai. He had nothing on underneath.

Marco knew the drug-induced heat required orgasm for relief, not the hormones in an alpha's seed, so his mind raced for a solution without actually touching him. "Kai, sweetheart?" Marco looked into Kai's unfocused eyes and his heart squeezed painfully.

"Hurts," Kai gasped and tried to roll over. Marco needed to get his shit together *right the fuck now* and he quickly used the shorts as a barrier between them. Kai pushed himself against Marco's thigh, squirming and groaning until he came. Marco helped himself to some tissues and continued stroking Kai's back, talking quietly to him, praying it would be enough. He gently rolled Kai over, rubbed Kai's belly and pressed gentle kisses on his head because it seemed to soothe him and his breathing evened out.

He glanced at his watch and tried to rouse a practically unconscious Kai. Eight minutes. They had eight minutes and then all hell would break loose. He had to get Kai safely out of here. He knew in order to do that he would have to wake him. "Kai? It's Marco. Do you know who I am?"

Kai opened his eyes and smiled dreamily. "Marco," he sighed.

24

"Sweetheart, we have to go. I hate to, but we're going to have to run. You need to get dressed."

Confusion entered Kai's gorgeous eyes and he blinked. Frowned. Tried to sit up and failed. Marco helped him. "Where am I?" he asked slowly, carefully, as if the answer was the last thing he wanted to hear.

"You're at Samson's pack house. And in about five minutes a van is going to crash through the gates. We need to be ready to run."

Alarm rushed into Kai's eyes and he practically threw himself out of bed. It took him a second to realize he was naked, a little cum still smeared on his belly. Marco saw the exact moment he became aware of what had happened. The disbelief, the *betrayal*, and then the coldness as everything in Kai shut down...or shut down to Marco. They didn't have time to say anything, but Marco doubted he could come up with words at that point anyway.

"Quick, we need to be ready." Marco reached out for Kai's arm as he swayed a little, but Kai firmed his jaw and yanked his arm out of Marco's grasp almost violently. Marco didn't get the chance to respond as they both heard the screech of tires, then saw headlights through the window. The engine revved before a loud crash echoed as the gates flew off their hinges.

"Now," Marco snapped ignoring Kai's protests and grabbed him, hustling him to the door. He opened it and heard shouting and the sound of running feet. He ducked back inside as a huge gamma ran past waving a gun. *Shit.* He hoped Ryker was ready for that.

"This way."

They both turned and saw Charles beckoning them frantically.

"No," Kai pulled back. "Don't trust him."

Marco registered the hurt in Charles's expression as he seemed to take a hit from the words, but making a split-second decision, Marco decided to trust him and yanked Kai after him and after Charles through a kitchen and out of a back door. Charles pointed to the fence. "You have to be quick. It will be another dealer."

"Don't trust him." Kai pleaded even as he swayed trying to remain upright.

"It isn't a dealer." Marco turned to Charles. "They're my friends. We came to rescue Kai. Come with us." Marco held out his other arm, but Charles shrank back away.

"I can't."

"Come with us. I can keep you safe." For a moment Charles's eyes widened with longing, but then they heard shouting from the kitchen.

"No. You go. I'll cover for you. If they think it was just me out here, they won't look for you at this side."

"Charles—" Marco started, but the shouts got louder as gunfire rang out.

Charles turned. "Get him to safety." And he ran back to the building.

Marco swore, but he didn't have any choice. They headed towards the east road and the dumpster area as previously arranged. He lifted Kai over the fence, ignoring Kai's protest, and spotted Ryker's dark blue truck. They both ran to it as the door opened. They jumped in as Chrissy yelled "I've got them" into her phone. She gunned the engine the moment Marco slammed the door closed.

Tires screeching, Chrissy headed for the entrance, made a hard right and put her foot down. Marco looked at Kai. "I need to check you over."

He pulled his medical bag from the floor and looked up to meet Kai's gaze.

"I'm fine."

"I just need—"

"You lay one finger on me and I'm out of this truck." He yanked at the blanket on the seat to cover himself up. Shame burned through Marco and he couldn't even meet Chrissy's eyes in the rearview mirror. Marco pulled off his jacket, stripped off his shirt and handed it to Kai without speaking. Kai hesitated then snatched it from him and quickly yanked it over his head. "I need to get Maddox," Kai whispered to Chrissy, completely ignoring Marco.

"Probably our next move," Chrissy said. "Let's meet up with Ryker and see what the plan is." Ryker called a moment later saying they were all okay and would meet them soon. Another fifteen minutes and she pulled up behind a gas station. A white Chevrolet pickup that was bashed in, and concerningly had a few bullet holes peppering the front, pulled in behind them.

Marco shot another look at Kai, but he was out of the truck and running to Ryker before Marco had taken his seat belt off. Chrissy turned to him and put a hand on his arm. "I'm guessing it was bad."

Marco just nodded, unwilling to say any more. Ryker and the others joined him a moment later, and Red pulled up in a black minivan.

Marco took a breath and got out. "There's a guy called Charles who helped—"

"Hold me down while they poured the crap into my mouth," Kai snapped. "He's one of Samson's."

Marco ignored Kai and looked at Ryker. "He got us out of the kitchen door. He thought a dealer war was starting. I tried to get him to come with us, but he ran back to distract them so we could get away. We might not have gotten to Chrissy as easily or at all without him."

"They had guns," Ryker confirmed. Kai opened his mouth to say something else but closed it and glanced at Ryker.

"I need to get Maddox."

"We need to get holed up and find out what info Zeke has gotten us," Ryker said.

"I—"

"We can't just walk in there, Kai. You know that," Ryker said gently. "Dealing with Karl Harker needs a completely different plan. He's clever, efficient and organized. Zeke is working on a trade. We have zero chance of getting Maddox by force."

Kai put his hand to his mouth and turned away. Marco wanted to comfort Kai with everything in him, but he knew it wasn't welcome. "Have you had a chance to check him over?"

Marco looked at Ryker. "No." He knew he meant Kai.

"Then both of you go to the minivan while I try and call Zeke."

Kai sent Marco a thunderous look, but Ryker simply said. "It's not up for debate, or I'll have someone take you back to the pack."

Kai turned and walked back to the van. Marco picked up his bag and followed. Kai sat looking out of the dark window and didn't turn when Marco climbed in. "So, was I begging for it?"

Marco jerked and paused at getting the blood pressure monitoring equipment out. "No. They'd given you too much. You were practically unconscious."

"And you got off on that, did you?"

Marco didn't bother replying. There was zero point. He was sorely tempted to justify his actions. To explain that Kai's life was in danger and no matter how much Marco hated being in that position, he had been on a clock. And because ultimately while he might have hated the circumstances, Marco had adored every second he had gotten to hold Kai. And that made him just as bad as the ones who had given the shit to Kai in the first place.

And even if it killed Marco, Kai hating him might be the only thing that would keep him safe.

That was the only thing that mattered.

Chapter Five

Kai didn't bother looking Marco in the face while he listened to his heartbeat and took his blood pressure. Marco undid the cuff from his arm. "Still a little high, but better." Kai didn't reply. He just wanted to curl up in a humiliated ball and never have to see him again. And as soon as he had Maddox he would leave. He didn't care where to. Marco packed his equipment away and got out of the car just as Ryker's phone rang.

"I will have to ask," Ryker said after a moment, then winced. He clicked the phone off and looked at Marco. "Apparently Samson isn't as stupid as I gave him credit for. He immediately called Harker when he realized you were both missing and that we had left without returning fire." Kai scrambled out of the minivan, still in Marco's shirt which hung down to his knees.

"And what does he want?" Chrissy asked.

"He hasn't said. Harker, however, wants to know how much Maddox is worth to you." Kai hissed in a breath. He had no money.

"Did he give him a figure?" Marco asked.

Ryker nodded. "Zeke is trying—"

"I'll pay. I can afford it." Marco gazed at Ryker and Kai risked a glance at him. Something unspoken seemed to pass between Marco and Ryker.

"How much has he asked for?" Kai asked.

Ryker glanced at him "A hundred thousand."

"Dollars?" Kai squeaked out and swayed, the buzzing in his ears insistent. Before he knew what was happening, he was sitting back on the edge of the seat, his head between his knees, Marco's firm hand rubbing his back.

"It'll be okay," Marco promised, but Kai knocked his hand away.

"I don't want your money."

Chrissy scowled. "Do you have any idea—" But Marco put a hand up to stop her.

"This doesn't obligate you. This is an emergency fund I'm donating to Zeke so he can use it to rescue any shifter. I was going to do it anyway. It's pure coincidence that Maddox is the first one to benefit."

Kai looked at Marco, guilt and discomfort swirling in his belly. He knew he was being a bitch. He felt like he had zero dignity left after last night, but his feelings weren't important right now. Maddox was important. "Thank you."

Marco simply stood. "I'll transfer the money to Zeke. Harker can't know where it came from." He took out his phone and stepped away. Kai sat up and accepted the bottle of water Chrissy handed him. They all heard Marco talking, issuing clipped instructions to someone. When he finished, he looked back at Ryker. "He's going to call us in a few minutes."

Kai clutched the bottle harder trying not to let his hands shake, his hazy memory sharpening a little as he pictured Marco's touch. He had tried to undo Marco's shirt and Marco had stopped him, but then he remembered being on a bed with Marco. Had Samson watched? It didn't make sense. He knew what it had felt like to take the omega stuff, but this time it had felt different. He hated Marco anyway. He could easily blame Marco for the fact he had had to leave the pack in the first place.

No, I can't. He wanted to. He *really* wanted to, but a small, insistent voice wouldn't let him. He didn't understand why. He got that Marco had been involved in the rescue. Completely understood he was the only one who would pass as human. He also understood he'd been given the stuff to make him horny, but Marco said he'd been practically unconscious. Had Marco just wanted to get him out of his system hoping he could get away with it, or had he been forced to put a show on for Samson? It must have been because Samson was there. It had to have been.

"Is he okay?" Red asked Marco.

"Yes, his blood pressure's a little high but that may be the added stress as well." Marco still didn't look at him. Ryker's phone rang and he answered it immediately.

"Good," Ryker responded. Kai's heart thudded when Ryker nodded, but then he frowned. "I'll ask." He looked at Marco. "He wants the 'human' to bring the cash. He won't accept an electronic trail."

Kai groaned inwardly.

"And to his pack house. No one else will be allowed there. Once the funds have been checked Marco gets to leave with Maddox."

There was a moment's silence. "Do you believe him?" Chrissy asked.

"We don't have a choice," Marco said.

Ryker tipped his head like he agreed. "Our only benefit is that Harker doesn't know you're a shifter."

"But won't they guess?" Kai said in frustration. "Panther shifters aren't rare."

"But having any dealings outside their clan is," Red got in before anyone else. "Every shifter knows the danger of mating a panther shifter. Emmett's grandma is very unusual."

"I'd be more willing to believe Marco was a human, especially given Zeke is a hundred percent human and the fact that the council knows about him and trusts him," Red said. "Human or not, Marco has an established background with the ranger service as a medic. Since when have panther shifters worked in any field that doesn't bring them in a shit ton of cash?"

He was right. And yet Kai still wanted to argue. He didn't though. He needed to focus on Maddox. The phone rang again and Ryker answered it. Kai watched as Ryker kept his gaze on Marco all the time. "Understood." He hung up.

"We have to lay low tonight. We're still a-ways from Harker's pack house and Zeke has to get the cash delivered to us. We have to give him a location to be able to do that." He looked at Kai. "And some of us need food and rest."

Kai didn't bother to express an opinion. He felt like everything was out of his hands. His life, Maddox's life, and their future. If they had one together, what that would look like? Could he go somewhere and pass as human? He wanted to go back to a pack, but didn't want to rely on an alpha to make that happen. He felt a brush on his arm and focused on Ryker. "We'll get him back. And there are a lot of shifters who are working to make sure this sort of thing never happens again. As soon as we have him, I'm naming you both pack."

Kai's eyes widened. "You can do that?"

"I was ratified as Alpha by the council and so was the pack. The pups too." Hope swirled in Kai. "You'd already left or I would have said. I'm sorry."

Kai launched himself at Ryker. He needed his alpha so very much then, and Ryker understood. He held him close. "Emmett tried to get ahold of you."

Kai stepped back. "I was trying to start again. I needed to be settled before I could—" he swallowed. "It's pathetic, but I couldn't bear to hear about other people being happy until I was." He heard a small, wounded sound behind him and turned. Marco looked like he'd been kicked...hard. Kai opened his mouth, but Marco whirled and walked away.

It isn't my fault. He had been Marco's for the taking. Now? Not so much. He felt Ryker's steadying arm around him. "Let's get you to the hotel. I'm surprised you're vertical to be honest."

Ryker had booked them into a generic hotel next to a truck stop which meant they would be left alone. All the shifters were mature enough that they could go for long periods of time without needing to let their animal out, but Kai had been assured that at least one of them would be in animal form and guarding the grounds all night. There were enough places a shifter could hide, and Ryker didn't want to get caught unawares. Kai was shown to his own room. It was simple, but clean. A moment later Chrissy arrived with takeout and water. She left him after encouraging him to rest.

Then he was alone. Alone and didn't want to be because he missed Maddox with such an intensity it felt like his skin was being scraped raw. He shivered despite the room being warm and curled up on the bed, drawing the comforter up. Tears that had been threatening for what seemed like forever quickly pooled in his eyes, but this time he didn't try and stop them. And of course, once he let go he couldn't seem to stop. Wary of whichever shifter's hearing that would be in the next room, he stuffed the comforter against his mouth to try and muffle the sobs. Concentrating on staying quiet while feeling like someone was taking a knife to his heart, he didn't hear the door open, just felt the bed dip and strong arms pull him close. Kai buried his head against the man he wanted to hate but simply couldn't and sobbed.

He opened his eyes sometime later at a tap on the door. He must have slept his first non-drugged sleep in days. He stumbled as he got up and opened it. Ryker looked tired but resolute. "We have the cash. Get ready and eat." He handed Kai a bag of snacks. "We're meeting at the cars in an hour." Kai nodded, incapable of words, and turned to the bed as Ryker left. The empty bed. Had he dreamed Marco being there? But Kai knew he hadn't. How had Marco known, and how had he gotten into the room? Kai's gaze slid to the door on the far wall and guessed it connected. He sat on the edge of the bed and pulled the other pillow towards him, pressing it to his face and inhaling. Could he smell Marco? Panthers didn't have a shifter scent, but Marco still smelled of Marco to him. Comfort and danger at the same time. And all man. Marco had held him while Kai had fallen apart last night. Held him, comforted him, then left when he had gone to sleep. Kai had no idea what to think about that at all. He didn't especially want to think about it.

Kai joined them at the cars. When he glanced at Marco, Marco was looking at Ryker intently while he was on the phone. "No way," Ryker clipped out.

"What is it?" Kai whispered, terrified of the answer.

"Let me talk to them," Ryker sighed, then looked up. "The exchange is set, but Harker has moved the goalposts."

"What does he want?" Chrissy asked.

"He wants Kai to go as well."

"No fucking way," Marco snapped out.

Kai gaped. His mind racing. "I—"

"It's the only deal on the table."

"It's not right," Marco railed. "I don't trust this bastard any further than I could throw him. Kai's been through enough."

"I can do this," Kai interrupted. "Maddox is my responsibility."

Marco stepped up to Ryker looking all the world like he was challenging his alpha. "You didn't see what they did to him last night. It would have been *rape*." Which silenced Kai and it seemed everyone else. What had actually happened? Were his memories screwy? He'd wanted Marco since the moment he'd laid eyes on him, but all he thought about now when their eyes met was hands on his body. And not the good kind. The ones that violated him. Samson watching. It was like Marco had taken every part he'd liked about himself and cheapened it. Not that he'd ever felt worth much, but right up until last night he'd had some self-respect. Now he didn't feel like he even had that. He'd taken chance after chance, convinced there was someone out there who would want him for him not just as a baby machine.

But he'd been wrong so many times.

"There's no choice," Kai said. "I have to get Maddox back."

"No," Marco ground out.

"It might be the only way at this point," Ryker said, defeated. Marco sighed, but then he looked right at Kai.

"Okay, but you have to promise me one thing." Kai nodded expecting all the warnings about doing as he was told, being careful.

"You have to promise me that no matter what happens you won't reveal I'm a panther."

Kai blinked stupidly. "Okay." Of everything he thought Marco was going to say, that wasn't on the list.

Marco stepped right into Kai's space. "I mean it. Maddox's life may depend on it."

"Maddox's life?" Kai parroted. "What on earth do you mean?"

"I mean," Marco said very quietly. "That if my Panthera found out

34

Baby and the Panther

about you she would have you killed. I cannot guarantee she would leave Maddox alone either."

"Killed," Kai repeated again. "But why?"

Marco lifted his hand and gently—ever so gently—trailed his fingers down Kai's cheek. "You know why."

Kai's throat nearly closed and he jerked his head back from temptation. He wanted to lean into Marco's touch so very badly. "I don't understand."

"Yes, you do," Marco said quietly, then stepped back. "Let's do this."

35

Chapter Six

Marco stared out of a car window for the second time in forty-eight hours, but this time he was driving. Kai was sitting quietly beside him, and an empty baby seat took pride of place in the back. Marco just prayed it was occupied when they returned. He knew Kai had a million questions and he didn't know how he was holding them all in. Marco would do this. Get Maddox. See they were both safe at the pack house. Then he would leave. He just couldn't risk her finding out about them. He wasn't even concerned if she found him. She knew Nicholas had untied him and driven him away. Only his brother would have dared go against the Panthera. He had two brothers and not one of them would normally have risked her displeasure, but Nicholas had come storming in and said she'd crossed a line. How Marco had even managed to stand was a miracle, but Nicholas had shifter strength. He had gotten Marco away, secured him in a motel where he could sleep off his injuries and shift, then he had put him on a plane.

Nicholas had saved his life. He wasn't ever sure if his mother wouldn't have come back and finished the job. He missed his little brothers, both of them. He had loved the twins when they were babies.

But that was in another life. A life he hadn't had to leave if he could have sucked it up. Funny, but that was one regret he'd never had right up until this moment. The thought he might be putting his mate in danger... No, he *knew* he was putting Kai in danger.

"So, what's the plan?"

Marco glanced at Kai. He'd been silent since they had gotten in the car, but his hands had been twisting nervously. Marco had been aware of every hurried breath. Every nervous swallow. "We drive to the gate house. We will be there in a few minutes." He paused because it needed repeating. "I can't stress how important it is that you don't tell them I'm a panther."

Kai looked out of the window. "So you said."

"Maddox—"

"I get it," Kai snapped. "He is the most important thing in my world. I know that I would give anything, do anything, to save him." He paused and lowered his voice. "I just wasn't expecting you to feel the same."

Marco didn't know what to say. There was nothing *to* say. So long as Kai believed Maddox was at risk it didn't matter. They just had to get through tonight. Another mile and Marco turned off. The lane was poorly lit, but he knew they would have been seen.

He stopped at a barrier and squinted as a light was shined into his eyes. Only for show as no shifter needed visual confirmation. They would smell them. For the millionth time Marco said thanks to the universe for making panther shifters undetectable by scent.

"Drive up to the first building."

The order was short and sweet, so Marco did as he was told. When he killed the engine in front of a very large house, they were surrounded by so many enforcers it was laughable. If Marco found any of this amusing that is.

He got out of Ryker's truck and waited for Kai, then they both walked forward following the not-so-subtle urging from the enforcers behind them. They were shown into a huge hall. The house itself was stunning. Turn of the century or gothic revival that Marco didn't really care for, but the staircase that Harker stood on was quite impressive. So were the huge windows. The red velvet drapes were a little too much. And he had to admit to being surprised. Most wolf shifters went with natural materials. Wood cabins, often very large ones, but not old-fashioned brick edifices from another age. He wasn't sure what Harker was trying to prove.

"I have the money."

Harker smiled and came down the stairs. He gestured for them to walk ahead of him into another room. "Let's not be so hasty. I was surprised to learn of your involvement with Coleman."

"He has a large organization," Marco acknowledged. "I got involved after a cave rescue." Which tied in nicely. As back stories went it was a good one.

"So I understand." Harker waved them into a large seating area. "What I'd like to know is, what's your interest in the omega?"

Marco's smile was brittle. "Coleman's organization is all about rescuing shifters, especially omegas." His tone and sarcasm didn't go unnoticed. "It's what we do," Marco added a little more conciliatory.

Harker turned his attention to Kai. "You could stay here. Maybe I was too hasty when I sold you. If your charms are such that you have someone willing to pay that sort of cash, then you must be something special."

"I just want to leave with Maddox," Kai whispered.

"Where is he? Can we get this completed?" Marco pushed.

"So, you're a medic," Harker carried on as if neither of them had spoken.

Marco knew what being played felt like, he'd had it done to him for years. "Can we get down to business?" He hefted the bag containing the cash. "I'm sure you want to count it."

Harker smiled, not rising to the bait at all. "Oh, I think I trust you."

"Well, I don't trust you, so how about you bring out the child?" He knew his name was Maddox. Of course he did. But he wanted Harker to keep believing this was a business transaction, that he wasn't personally involved.

"I might have changed my mind," Harker said almost casually. Kai couldn't contain the quickly indrawn breath they all heard. "Oh, no, you can have the kid, I just decided there's something else I want for him."

Harker waved a hand. A she-wolf appeared a moment later with a sleeping Maddox. Kai stood, wanting to reach for him immediately. After she received a look from Harker signaling permission, Kai had Maddox in his arms. For a second Marco got lost in the look of love in Kai's eyes when he held his son. The completeness. Whatever Harker wanted, it was worth it.

"You have your money." Marco stood as if Harker hadn't spoken at all. Harker chuckled, but it was such a harsh sound Marco knew it was false.

"Not so fast."

And then, before Marco could blink, ten enforcers surrounded them. Marco fisted his hands and tried to breathe.

"What do you want?" he ground out.

"Maybe I want a pack medic," Harker trilled.

By not one flicker of an eyebrow would Marco show Harker he'd been waiting for something just like this.

"I'll discuss it when the omega and his child leaves." He ignored the stunned look from Kai.

"But then all your incentive disappears. Please," Harker continued. "Do you think I'd be so careless?" It was a rhetorical question.

Marco could think of a hundred different replies to that. He settled for a shrug. "Your choice." He would do anything to get Kai and Maddox to safety, but he couldn't let Harker know that.

Another enforcer entered the room and hurried up to Harker, bending and whispering in his ear. Marco's hearing was exceptionally acute and he definitely caught the word Samson.

"It seems we have a challenge for ownership," Harker almost purred out.

"For Maddox?" Marco frowned. He didn't dare look at Kai. Harker waved a hand.

"No. I'm happy with the deal. You can take the spawn as soon as you like." Marco turned and urged Kai to move. He didn't want the bastard having any opportunity to change his mind.

Kai turned as well, his arms tight around Maddox as if he was expecting someone to rip the baby from his arms. From what Marco understood, that was what had happened last time. So if the challenge—Marco cut off the thought. *Shit.* Of course the challenge wasn't for Maddox.

It was for *Kai*.

And as if Marco had conjured him, a snarling, furious Samson stomped into the room. "You," he yelled pointing at Marco. He turned to Harker. "The omega is mine. Rightfully paid for. I demand his return."

Harker arched a challenging eyebrow at Marco. "We do seem to have a problem."

"How much?" Marco asked trying to tamp down his animal's reaction to simply pick up his mate and run. With the enforcers in the room, he doubted they would make it to the door. And Kai or Maddox could be hurt.

"I don't want the money. I want the omega." Samson was pissed. And worse, they'd underestimated him. They'd counted him as some patsy of Harker and not a real threat. It wasn't Marco's biggest mistake ever, but he knew it would be his last one.

Harker opened his hands, palms up in a "what am I supposed to do" gesture.

"I will double whatever you gave," Marco said.

Samson scoffed. "I paid for a fucking omega. He's *mine*."

"I'm assuming," Harker added almost as if it was an afterthought. "You don't have a spare omega to offer up instead. Samson might consider a swap accompanied by the right financial incentive."

Of course he fucking didn't, but then he caught the smug look Samson couldn't successfully hide when he looked at Harker. It was a set up. Samson was doing Harker's bidding. The fact that it didn't alter anything was ridiculous. "Triple."

Kai's gasp was audible and for the first time Marco turned and met Kai's eyes. His beautiful, completely breathtaking ones. Kai was his. He'd always been his.

"No," Samson said.

Marco ignored him. His gaze stayed locked on Kai's for another moment. He took in Kai's terror and confusion and sent back security and warmth. All without saying one word. He registered when Kai got it as he relaxed a little. Held Maddox close. "You promised," he mouthed, and knew from the widening of Kai's eyes he understood what Marco was referring to. That he wouldn't ever reveal what Marco was.

Marco turned and matched the cocky smirks in front of him with an implacable expression. He saw Harker's gaze sober as he took in Marco's grim determination and saw when the thought registered that he might have underestimated Marco. Marco glanced at Samson.

"Then I issue a formal mate challenge."

Samson gaped. Even Harker looked non-plussed for a second before he recovered. Samson stammered. "B-But you're human."

"And a member of the Blue Ridge Pack, ratified by the council. My alpha as I'm sure you are aware is a hybrid."

Harker didn't reply. Just narrowed his eyes. But Marco knew even Harker couldn't deny him this. The council would enforce it and Harker enjoyed the fact that he always skirted just under their radar.

"Fine," snapped out Samson and Marco held his hand up.

"I demand seconds present to ensure the fight is fair."

Harker's jaw worked and Marco had a brief moment of satisfaction that things weren't going Harker's way all of a sudden. "You do understand they can't interfere?" Marco nodded at Harker who sighed and spoke to his enforcers. Ryker and the team were waiting in the other car just beyond the pack boundary. It would take five minutes, if that, for them to get here. Maddox woke and started fussing. Marco turned to Harker.

"We need a diaper and some milk." Harker waved a disinterested hand and in another moment the same female who had brought Maddox reappeared and beckoned Kai. Kai glanced at Marco and he nodded. He would prefer the challenge be done without Kai there, but he knew that wasn't possible.

"You're an odd human," Harker said after a few minutes silence with the same inflection he might use for commenting about the weather. "You do know you will die?"

Marco didn't bother answering what was clearly a rhetorical question and at the same time Ryker and the rest of the team walked in.

Harker settled back in his seat. "Your human has issued a mate challenge."

Ryker met Marco's steady gaze. For a second, complete understanding passed between them. Ryker knew Marco would give his life for Kai. And

Marco understood—hoped—Ryker would get Kai to safety. At least if Marco wasn't a complication, Ryker could involve the Panthera, Emmett's grandmother. His own mother might be a Panthera, but she wouldn't stand a chance against Regina.

Ryker took charge because Harker didn't seem to care one way or another, but then he probably didn't. On the surface Marco had no hope against a wolf, even one as pathetic as Samson. Well, he was going to prove him wrong.

"Submission or death." Ryker stated formally which was unnecessary. There was only one way a mate challenge would go. Marco nodded and Samson shifted. It was pathetic. The change didn't happen swiftly or painlessly. If Marco had shifted into his cat, he would have been a sleek killing machine while Samson was still thinking about it. Except he couldn't. For this he was a hundred percent human and even against a pathetic wolf, maybe a hundred percent screwed. Except Marco had been fighting all his life. And this was a fight he had to win.

Kai walked back into the room and Chrissy tugged him to her. Marco shot one last look at Kai and his heart eased. He could almost see the mate bond as a physical presence even though technically they still needed to join. Not that even that that was likely to happen now. Somehow he had to defeat Samson, or stay alive long enough for Ryker to have a back-up plan, because the promise that had arced between them told Marco that Ryker wouldn't leave Kai. He didn't honestly know what Ryker had done but he knew it was something.

"Give the child to the she-wolf," Harker ordered and Kai took a step back into Chrissy.

"No."

"Your choice. Either surrender him or the challenge is forfeit."

Maddox whimpered and Marco's heart ached to comfort him even as one of the enforcers snatched Maddox out of Kai's hands. Chrissy had to physically restrain Kai from going after the enforcer. At that moment, Marco caught movement out of the corner of his eye. He had barely a second to react as Samson launched himself—all two hundred pounds of him —at Marco.

Chapter Seven

Kai clung to Chrissy. The enforcer passed Maddox to the she-wolf and she at least stepped closer to him. He heard the snarl and the crash as furniture toppled from the center of the room, and more enforcers cleared things out of the way. Harker didn't move. He didn't look troubled in the slightest. There was nothing Kai could do except watch, and he knew in his heart of hearts that Marco was in trouble. He knew he wouldn't shift. He'd made that clear. But a human against a wolf? The chances of Marco coming out alive were slim. He glanced pleadingly at Chrissy, but all her attention was on the battle in front of her. A pained grunt was all Marco allowed himself as an arc of blood sprayed across the floor. Kai battled not to close his eyes, he knew whose blood that was. Surely Ryker would stop it. Marco was still on his feet and circling the wolf. A gaping slice of skin ran down his rib cage and blood splattered the floor. Kai moaned. He had to do something. He had to. He couldn't let Marco die, no matter what he'd promised.

"Alpha," Kai begged Ryker and Ryker glanced at him without expression, then subtly moved so Kai and Maddox were behind him. Then he nodded to Chrissy and Red, and they tensed. Kai couldn't breathe. He knew they were about to interfere, but against the fifty plus enforcers Harker had?

Marco was fast, incredibly so in his unshifted form and somehow he twisted behind Samson and took him to the floor, his arm in a lock around the wolf's neck. Kai held his breath. No human could defeat a wolf, surely? But for a seemingly endless second, Marco looked like he was winning.

An enforcer came rushing into the room and headed for Harker. He listened to another few words and held up his hand for the fight to stop. Kai gasped out a shaky breath. Marco released Samson and the wolf gasped and choked, rolling away. Marco got to his feet, but he'd lost a lot of blood and it was still dripping. They just had to get him to somewhere he could shift and he would be okay. Harker snarled and tried to pin Ryker with his gaze. "Why the fuck have I got a panther claw at my perimeter and a Panthera threatening to take me out?"

Kai laughed a little hysterically and turned just as he saw Samson tense. "Marco," Kai screamed in warning, but he was a fraction of a second too late to stop Samson from lunging and raking Marco with his claws. Blood sprayed everywhere, gushing from the fresh wound on his neck. Marco crashed to the floor under Samson as the doors opened and suddenly the room was full of panther shifters. *Very full.* But Kai took no notice and neither did Ryker or Chrissy. They both hoisted Samson off an unconscious Marco as the Panthera—Emmett's grandmother—walked elegantly into the room on three-inch heels. Kai collapsed to his knees trying ineffectually to stop the blood loss. "Marco," he whispered brokenly, but without another word the Panthera knelt beside him and touched Marco's head. In his place a sleek black cat lay motionless and then that form was replaced by Marco. A completely naked Marco.

"The fuck," Harker snarled and struggled against the two panther shifters holding him effortlessly.

She completely ignored him, turned and levelled her gaze on Kai. "He is your mate?"

Kai nodded wordlessly. She extended one well-manicured hand and cupped Kai's face. She smiled. Marco's eyes were closed but he was breathing. "You will need to be brave. You will both be in danger, possibly out of my control."

"I don't care so long as Marco's okay."

She eyed him carefully and Kai let her look her fill. "Very well." She stood and turned to Harker and Samson, both restrained by members of her claw. Kai didn't even want to think about what had happened to the rest of Harker's enforcers. "You are both stripped of your packs. All of your assets have been seized by the council and you are coming with me."

"You fucking bitch," Harker snarled. "I'll have your hide."

She simply arched an eyebrow looking bored. "Bigger men than you have tried."

Kai sat in the back of Ryker's truck all the way home. On one side Maddox was secure in his baby seat, fed, changed and asleep. On the other side Marco was stretched out, covered by a blanket, his head resting on Kai's lap, also asleep. Regina had assured them all that Marco just needed to sleep. A Panthera could force a shift in all panthers to heal wounds, similar to a wolf Alpha, but she couldn't replace blood loss. Marco needed a couple of days rest, some food and plenty of care. Kai had every intention of delivering just that.

Marco woke bleary eyed after about four hours and Ryker and Red helped him to the bathroom to get dressed and use the facilities. Kai had itched to help, but Marco was simply too big for him to be of any use. So he saw to Maddox, silently thanking the fates he was an easy baby. When Marco returned with Ryker, Kai could see the strain on his face and the line of sweat that dotted his brow. He squeezed back in as close to the baby seat as possible to give Marco room and Marco got back in. Kai took Marco's hand. They needed to talk, but they needed to be alone to do that. He wasn't letting Marco go though, whatever the stubborn panther thought. Marco didn't seem inclined to argue and he just rested their entwined hands on his lap. Another mile and Marco was trying to force his eyelids to stay open, so Kai simply turned and angled his back to the car seat and tugged Marco back against him. Marco stopped fighting and slept the rest of the way home.

Kai even dozed a little, but his thoughts were full of where he was going to stay when they got back to the pack. He wanted to be with Marco, but he didn't know what Marco wanted. And what about Maddox?

A chill ran down Kai's arms. *Maddox.* Maddox wasn't Marco's. They might be mates, but they hadn't bonded so neither would get sick if they weren't together. Some shifters—some humans—didn't welcome children from someone else. And what about the whole panther thing? There was something else going on that Kai didn't understand.

He opened his eyes and met Ryker's briefly in the mirror. Ryker sent him a gentle smile before he focused back on the road, but Kai still fretted for the next hour until they got home. The road to the pack house was bumpy enough to wake both Maddox and Marco. Marco sat up. Kai didn't know whether Marco was deliberately distancing himself, but Maddox had worked himself into a fit as they pulled in. Dinah, Zeke, and Fox were waiting for them. Marco got out of the car very stiffly. Kai ached to help, but he needed to get Maddox unbuckled before he started screaming.

"I've got your new room all ready," Dinah said comfortingly. Kai lifted Maddox into his arms and Maddox quieted immediately. Kai inhaled Maddox's baby smell and his heart settled. They were safe. Maddox was safe, and sudden tears wet his lashes.

"Let's get you inside. Why don't you give Maddox to me and—"

Kai instinctively jerked away from Dinah's outstretched arms. There was a brief silence. "I'm sorry," Kai said wretchedly.

"I understand," Dinah said. "I'd feel exactly the same. Let me show you to your room." Kai followed Dinah into the pack house. *Your* room, not their room. He knew they were going in the direction of the omega rooms and felt a little better they were inside rather than in one of the cabins. He'd been ready for his independence the first time he had arrived, but now it was the last thing he wanted. All these rooms were connected so they could be made into bigger spaces if an omega had more than one child. He got a glimpse of Ryker and Marco as Ryker shut the door they walked past. Dinah opened the next door. Kai's heart beat a little faster. Marco was in the room next door? He glanced at Dinah and she smiled knowingly.

Then he looked at the room and bit his lip hard. He was going to cry. "Hey." He whirled around, saw Emmett standing in the doorway and simply burst into tears. Another moment and he and Emmett had Maddox stuck between them as they hugged each other. Maddox protested immediately and they broke apart laughing. "You did this." Kai waved at the gorgeous room. The crib and mobile. The bottle warmer and changing station. He could see soft baby toys all stacked up and knew for sure the dresser would be full of clothes. His bed looked so comfy, covered in a snuggly comforter and extra throws. There was even a rocking chair in the corner where he could feed Maddox, and a baby monitor.

"Of course I did," Emmett said and kissed Maddox's head. "I was just putting Josie down or we would have both been outside to meet you."

"I can't wait to see her," Kai admitted.

Emmett beamed. "I'm so happy you're home." He waggled his eyebrows. "We omegas have to stick together." Kai nodded eagerly. "You get yourself settled and I'm going to get you some food."

"I can get it." Emmett had only given birth himself three days ago. Emmett didn't bother replying just waved it off.

The room seemed quiet after Emmett left. Kai laid Maddox down in his crib and Maddox seemed to be suitably entertained by experimentally kicking his feet and stuffing a fist in his mouth. The door to the small bathroom was ajar and Kai smiled as he saw Emmett had been busy in there too. Large fluffy towels were lined up and there was a cute basket full of different kinds of soaps and lotions. He ran a hand over his jaw. He barely shaved twice a week, but Emmett had even remembered to leave him a shaving kit.

When he turned around, he was surprised to see Chrissy follow Emmett in with a tray full of food. Kai wasn't sure how hungry he was but he smiled and thanked Emmett. He got another hug before Emmett left, plus a promise to meet for breakfast the next morning. Chrissy placed a cell phone and charger on his nightstand.

47

"It's preprogrammed with a dozen numbers for people here," she said quietly.

"Thank you. I'm so grateful you came for me."

Chrissy smiled and glanced at the connecting door to Marco's room, then back at Kai. She didn't say a word, but Kai felt uncomfortable even after she left. What was that about? Did she blame Kai for Marco's injuries?

He sat down on the bed disconsolately. Did everyone blame him? Did Marco? What would it be like seeing Marco every day, but not being together.

You know why.

It had been Marco's answer when Kai had asked him why he was willing to risk his life for Maddox, but that could be just because he was a good guy. He was a medic, part of the rescue team. Nowhere in that phrase was the word *mate*. Kai had told the Panthera they were mates, but Marco hadn't said that.

And was it even a good idea? Did he trust himself not to make another mistake? And there wasn't just him this time. There was Maddox as well. He closed his eyes briefly as the memory of Maddox been yanked out of his arms played on a repeat in his head.

He looked over at the food, but his throat seemed to close at the thought of eating any of it. He'd eaten a protein bar that morning and an apple a little later. No one had given him grief for it because they were all nervous. Maddox experimented with a few gurgles and he kicked his legs furiously. Kai was exhausted, but he knew after sleeping so long in the car it would be a while before Maddox was ready to sleep again. He turned on the mobile above the crib and it started to play a quiet tune. Maddox seemed fascinated and Kai ran a soft finger down his cheek. Maddox automatically turned and reached for it. Kai huffed. "You can't possibly be hungry again."

The knock at the connecting door surprised Kai. "Come in." He expected Ryker but Marco stood there looking as washed out as earlier. Kai frowned. "You should be resting."

Marco huffed. "You sound like Fox. I think watching Josie's birth has him turning into a grandmother."

Kai felt a moment of envy which was ridiculous. Emmett deserved to be happy and surrounded by family. He turned away to get his voice under control. Kai had been alone when Maddox was born. The pack mother had come in as he delivered and briskly made sure Maddox and Kai were fine, helped him clean up and get Maddox settled, then left him to it. It wasn't that they were mean, it was just they all seemed to be on edge. And he remembered how Shaun had known Harker. Had he been worried then? Then why on earth had he brought an omega into the pack?

Or was it even though Shaun had seemed kind, he thought the same as others that omegas were disposable.

"How's Maddox?"

"He seems fine," Kai replied inadequately, still not looking at Marco. Marco stepped right up to the crib and turned Kai around to face him. Kai swallowed with difficulty and tried to lower his head, but Marco lifted his chin with a gentle finger. Wordlessly he thumbed the tears from Kai's cheeks, but Kai was helpless not to replace them with fresh ones. With a hurt, almost exasperated sound Marco drew Kai into his arms. Kai burrowed his head against Marco's chest and clung on. He'd dreamed of this for weeks. Marco ran a soothing hand up and down his spine. Kai shivered and pressed even closer.

"I'm so sorry."

"So am I." But apologizing didn't make everything magically better, or even different. *You know why.* Marco could just feel guilty. Maddox gurgled and tried to kick at the mobile. Kai stepped back and they drew apart. Marco turned to Maddox and murmured soothingly to him. "Any concerns?"

Kai shook his head. "He's amazing. He's sleeping six hours through the night."

Marco smiled. "There are a lot of new parents who would hate you right about now." Kai knew he'd been lucky in that. "I'd like you to bring him to the clinic tomorrow so I can give him a proper exam, but he seems fine."

And then it seemed awkward. He didn't know what to say. Marco made a frustrated sound and reached out again for Kai pulling him close. "I should let you go, but I'm just not strong enough."

Kai clung on. "Harker saw the Panthera make you shift. If Maddox is in danger, the safest place for us both is here."

"I know," Marco said quietly. "I tried. It was the hardest thing I ever did, watching you walk away." Marco moved at the same time as Kai looked up and their eyes met. Heat flared between them and it took nothing to bridge the gap as Kai pressed his lips to Marco's.

It was every bit as perfect as Kai knew it would be. The taste. The smell. The warm glide of Marco's lips against his and the insistent press of his tongue for entrance that Kai gave so willingly. Marco slid his palms up Kai's shirt and Kai thrilled at the touch of Marco's fingers against his bare skin.

A shrill cry broke them apart and Kai flushed. "I'm sorry. He slept a long time in the truck." But Marco didn't step back and let Kai manage, he stepped over to the crib and slid his arms under Maddox, gently lifting him up. Maddox seemed surprised, but he reached out a curious hand. Marco settled him against his chest and glanced at Kai who stood completely unable to wrench his eyes from either of them.

"Milk?" Marco prompted and Kai rushed over to get some pre-prepared bottles from the mini fridge that Emmett had shown him and put one in the warmer. Marco lifted Maddox up and in the time-honored tradition smelled his diaper and winced.

Kai rushed over feeling his cheeks flame. "I've got it."

Marco shrugged. "I don't mind," and he proceeded to efficiently and carefully change Maddox. By the time Maddox was clean, his bottle was ready. Kai tested the temperature, then reached out for Maddox automatically. Marco surrendered him, but then Kai wasn't sure where to sit. Marco sat on the bed against the pillows and widened his legs patting the covers between them. In almost a daze Kai handed Maddox to Marco then shuffled onto the bed, resting his back to Marco's chest. Marco handed Maddox back to him, then cocooned in Marco's arms, Kai settled back and fed Maddox.

"Did he get weighed at birth?"

Kai blinked. They were going to have a normal conversation when Kai's whole world had turned on its head? "Five pounds seven ounces."

"That's big for an omega baby," Marco said approvingly then hesitated. "I'm sorry I missed it, and I know I haven't said, but I'm sorry Danvers died."

Kai sighed. "I think he would have been kind. He—he gave me chance to settle in. I don't think either of us would have pretended we were mates, but he hadn't touched me." Marco seemed to relax a little more. "How do you feel?" Kai asked.

"Fine," Marco said. "Maybe a little tired," he allowed.

"I don't know what to say," Kai said hesitantly looking up at him. "You —" But Marco put a finger across Kai's lips.

"Forced you into a corner. We both knew we were mates and if I had stepped up you wouldn't have felt you had to leave. It was my fault you left your friends. Not yours."

Kai heaved out a breath. *Knew they were mates?* Did Marco *know* though? Kai watched Maddox's eyes close even though he still sucked furiously. Kai didn't think it would take much for him to join his son. He leaned his head back against Marco's chest and relaxed.

Kai jolted awake in what seemed like only a second later when he felt Maddox being lifted from his arms. His heart thudding painfully.

"It's only me," Marco said quietly. "You were both asleep. I was just going to put Maddox back in his crib." Kai looked down. Marco had slid his hands under the baby, but he'd not attempted to move anymore when Kai had panicked.

Kai let him go. "I'm sorry," Kai said quietly trying to explain. "We were made to go in the pack circle. Harker killed Shaun in front of us and then announced the auction. What about Esme?" Kai felt dreadful. He'd completely forgotten.

"She's in the same pack as her son. Ryker said the alpha has been warned, but apparently her son is being treated okay so they're both staying for the moment." Kai nodded. "What happened then?"

51

"Samson said he wanted an omega but wouldn't take someone else's brat." Kai bit his lip. "They knocked me out when I tried to get to him." Marco straightened from the crib, his face thunderous.

"I'm not surprised you reacted like that to me trying to take him. It will take a while to get through something like that." His face softened. "Why don't you go to the bathroom and I'll watch him for you?"

Kai warmed right through. Marco understood. He hadn't thought Kai was overreacting or pathetic or the million other scenarios he was expecting. He went into the bathroom with relief, but yawning, he didn't linger very long.

When he came out Marco looked up from the crib. Maddox was out for the count. "You look exhausted," he said softly. "Why don't you get into bed? I can leave my door open so I'll hear if you call."

Kai didn't breathe. He wanted Marco to stay with such an intensity it seemed to strip his need for everything else away. Even oxygen. *Dare he?* "Or you could sleep in here?"

For a moment Marco was so quiet Kai wasn't even sure he had heard him. "Would that make you feel safer?" Marco asked carefully, very carefully.

Kai considered what Marco was asking. Safer? He wanted to know if Kai just wanted him for security. He honestly didn't know. He felt like he didn't know anything anymore. He'd been sure in the car but now it was as if he didn't trust himself. "I always feel safer when I'm with you. I want to be close to you. I just mean sleep," he added. He didn't know if either of them were ready for more.

Marco smiled and stroked his cheek wondrously as if he couldn't believe what Kai was saying. "I'll be right back." Kai got into bed and lay down. He heard Marco opening a drawer and then the toilet flush in his bathroom and closed his eyes. In another moment, the covers lifted and Marco got in next to him. Kai was going to turn around to face him, but Marco just threw an arm across his waist and tugged him close to his chest. "Go to sleep, sweetheart," he murmured and dropped a kiss on his head.

Warm and wrapped up in Marco's arms, Kai didn't need to be asked twice.

Chapter Eight

He was hard. Not that Marco was surprised. He'd opened his eyes wondering what was pinning him down only to find his gorgeous mate sprawled out over him. Marco's cock was pushing into Kai's hip so much it was a wonder he hadn't woken up. Kai murmured and scratched his nose absently. Marco almost laughed. The hairs on his chest were clearly tickling Kai's nose. Marco tried to ease him over a little. He loved the feel of Kai sprawled over him, but he needed to be away from temptation. He moved him an inch over and closed his eyes firmly telling his traitorous body to behave. Then he noticed Kai's breathing had changed. "Did I wake you? Sorry." He bent and kissed his hair. Kai made an approving sound and wriggled his hips. Marco bit his lip to stop a groan from escaping. He wasn't sure Kai was properly awake, and knew his body could be responding before his brain kicked into action.

Marco opened his eyes again knowing there was no way he could go back to sleep. When Maddox had woken a couple of hours ago, Marco had prepared the bottle, then taken both of them in his arms while Maddox drank. He doubted if either of Maddox or Kai were still awake when the milk was finished. He quickly went to the bathroom, then snuggled back up to Kai. Maddox was a superstar and stayed asleep.

Kai wriggled again and a groan escaped Marco's throat. That seemed to wake Kai up properly. In the dim light from the baby monitor, even before dawn, he could see Kai's eyes open and fix on his. He bent and brushed a kiss over his lips, his cheek, his neck, any patch of skin he could reach. He felt the effect on Kai through his sleep shorts. A shiver seemed to run down Kai's arms. "Are you cold?"

Kai shook his head and arched his neck invitingly. Marco knew it was for more kisses, but still his blood surged at the innocent invitation. It would take nothing for Marco to deliver the mating bite, and he suddenly wanted nothing more than to bind Kai to him forever. He kept his fangs contained with difficulty, and nuzzled and licked the spot on Kai's neck. Needing more, he caught Kai's lips, sucking and licking, scraping tongues until Kai's shudders started being accompanied by gasps and quiet pleas.

"What do you need?" Marco got out, wanting confirmation that Kai knew what he was doing.

"You," Kai moaned. "Everywhere."

Marco smiled but he understood what Kai meant. He wanted nothing more than to live and breathe Kai. Be inside him. His dick throbbed painfully as if agreeing wholeheartedly and he reached down to check Kai. Kai groaned and pushed his slick, pulsing cock into Marco's fist. Marco let go and rolled him over, pinning Kai underneath him. The gasp and moan told Marco that Kai was happy to be pinned. To be caught. He felt underneath Kai's tight sac and his fingers swirled in Kai's omega slick. Good. That told him Kai was feeling this as much as he was. He slid one finger into Kai's heat and Kai shuddered, clamping down. "More."

Marco took his time though. He knew omegas were made for their mate, but he wouldn't ever risk a second of pain or discomfort. "Please," Kai begged. "Please."

Marco lined himself up, lifting Kai's ass up a little with his other hand and pushed in. Kai arched his head back, thrusting his hips so much Marco slid inside. Marco echoed Kai's groan and fisted his hands in the sheet. The feeling of being inside Kai was indescribable and for the first time in a very long time Marco was losing control.

He carefully slid back, almost to the tip, and thrust once more. Kai gave a low cry he tried to muffle. "Marco, again." So, Marco did. Far be it from him to deny his gorgeous mate even one second of pleasure.

Marco's head was spinning. Kai's taste, Kai's smell. The hot slick channel that tightened around Marco's dick promised nirvana and tempted him on and on. Marco was barely aware of his fangs descending, his sleek normally controlled cat wanting to take control of the little spitfire underneath him. He scraped Kai's skin just under his ear and Kai stiffened.

"No," the barely held panic in Kai's voice should have sent huge red flags to Marco's brain, but Kai pushed back just as Marco thrust and cried out. Pleasure thundered through every cell in his body. Kai cried out and collapsed underneath him and Marco followed him into oblivion.

The second cry Marco became aware of was from Maddox. He bent his head, too exhausted to move. Shit. They'd woken the baby. It might have been funny. He hated frightening Maddox, but he had to smile a little.

It took Marco a minute to soften. Kai tried to move, but Marco dropped a kiss on his cheek. "I got him." He slid out and grabbed a couple of tissues, hushing Maddox as he used a baby wipe on his hands, then he had the little scrap in his arms. Maddox quieted immediately and Marco simply got back into bed and laid Maddox on a pillow in between them both.

Kai raised exhausted but happy eyes to Marco and took Maddox's tiny hand in his and kissed it. "Sorry."

Marco took Kai's other hand. "Don't apologize. I imagine parents the world over have had moments like this." He turned Kai's hand over and kissed his palm. "I'll get his bottle. You stay there." He looked at the scratch on Kai's neck. He'd moved just in time when he'd registered that Kai refused the mating bite. Marco's mind raced with possible explanations. Had he panicked? Not that he'd be surprised if that was the case. They needed to talk about it, really talk. Kai had been through an awful lot in the space of a few weeks and the likelihood he was traumatized would surprise no one.

If he had been a wolf, Marco would have been the alpha, but clans didn't work like that. Which reminded him he needed to see if he could gain an audience with Emmett's grandmother. Ryker seemed to be able to call her whenever he wanted, and as Emmett's mate that didn't surprise him, but as a panther shifter, Marco knew he may be expected to observe clan etiquette. If he had to take Kai and hide, they would, but Kai was happy here. And Kai refusing the bite meant they weren't bonded. Which also meant Kai could leave. Leaving his mate might make him feel like he had the flu for a few weeks, but it wouldn't kill him.

For a moment he watched Kai. He didn't know what to say. He made the milk quickly and came back to bed. Kai still looked completely blissed out and Marco was cat enough to be pleased he was responsible. He waved the bottle. "May I?"

Kai beamed in response and Marco settled down, lifting Maddox. After testing the milk, he settled in to feed him. It took a minute before he realized Kai was quiet, and he glanced over to see Kai watching them both intently. Another ten minutes and Maddox was asleep again.

"I can't believe how good he is," Marco said. "Gemma from the rangers had twins and they never slept. Her mom had to move in with them because Gemma was making herself sick."

Kai smiled. "I know. I can't believe it myself." Marco settled Maddox back in his crib.

"I think we need to talk."

Kai nodded as if he'd been expecting it. They needed to talk about what exactly was wrong, but Marco felt he had to start at the beginning.

"I told you I'm running—was running—from my clan?"

"Not in so many words, but you never told me why."

"Because the one thing panther shifter clans—traditional ones—hate is mixed mating either with a human or another shifter. It started simply because the clans always thought they were superior and didn't want the bloodlines diluting. In a way that was self-prophesying because of the dire problem all shifters are having with the low birth rate."

Kai came closer and laid his head on Marco's chest. Marco played with Kai's hair. Somehow it was easier to talk about this when Kai was touching him.

"About fifteen years ago, I did something incredibly foolish. I'd lived a very sheltered life. When I reached twenty-one, I was suddenly given a nice house, a car and *freedom*. I quickly fell for an older man—James—that

I'd met in a bar. He was attentive, persuasive and I was convinced we were in love, so I told him what I was." He'd been so naive. "I was stupid, but I believed James when he said he loved me. I thought he was a writer and technically he was. What I didn't know was that he was a journalist and knew this story would make his career. I'd even shifted for him. He'd taken a snap on his phone before I had the chance to stop him, but it just showed my cat. It wasn't a video so he couldn't prove what I was."

Marco rubbed his head remembering the blows. "He decided to publish anyway. I hadn't realized what he'd actually found out. How secretive the clan was. Names, places. He'd even gotten a video of the Panthera getting into a car with two fully shifted panthers jumping into the back." Marco pulled Kai even closer. "And the Panthera had him killed. She had me tortured for three days until my brother found me and got me away."

Kai raised worried eyes. "I'm so sorry you were hurt. But what about the rest of your family? Couldn't they stop her? Your mom and dad even?"

Marco let out a deep sigh. "My mother is the Panthera of the whole of California, Nevada, and Arizona, but she has ambitions to be so much more." Kai's eyes widened and his mouth fell open. "She was the one who tortured me along with her personal enforcers. And the ridiculous thing was that what really upset her was censure from the shifter council. She was expecting to be made the leader of the whole thing, but I blew it for her. The story was suppressed easily enough, but my mom would never forgive my betrayal."

"And that's why?" Kai said. "Why you wouldn't acknowledge me, *us*?"

"I might have placed you in great danger. I'm going to talk to Ryker and Emmett's grandmother to see what I can do." Marco paused. "Is that why you wouldn't let me mark you?"

Kai was silent for so long Marco wasn't sure he was ever going to answer. "I just need some time. I've made so many mistakes and I don't want to hurt you, but I have to protect Maddox. It's different now. It's not just me."

"And I rejected you already, why should you trust me?"

Kai bent and kissed Marco's chest. "It's not so much that I don't trust you," Kai said. "It's that I don't trust myself. I've been wrong so many times.

I need to make sure Maddox is safe." And Marco couldn't guarantee that. He'd proved he was willing to give his life for both of them, but what if that wasn't enough? Marco had one more thing he had to say. That needed to be said.

"I wanted you to know something else. I'm not sure what you remember of the evening at Samson's, but I never did anything in front of him. I kept you close but he didn't see anything. I waited until we were alone."

Kai stilled. Marco waited an agonizingly long moment for his reply.

"But I remember"—he swallowed—"coming. Wasn't Samson there then?"

Marco shook his head. "No. You got off, but he was never in the room. I would never do that to you. You were barely conscious. I didn't want you imagining scenarios that never happened." Marco smiled tentatively, but his heart sank when Kai didn't return it. Still looking at the covers and avoiding Marco, Kai sat up.

"I'm going to grab a shower while Maddox is asleep." He moved quickly, avoiding the hand Marco stretched out.

"Kai?" He shouldn't have brought it up. "I'm sorry," he said quietly. "I just didn't want you to think you had people watching."

"No," Kai murmured and clutching the sheet in front of him, he moved to the bathroom. Marco's eyes narrowed. Kai wasn't shy.

"What's wrong?"

Kai raised his head and stared at Marco. Marco almost shivered. Gone was the sated happy expression, the teasing glances and the loving looks. "I want you to leave."

"What?" Marco scrambled out of bed. "What do you mean?"

"How could you?" Kai whispered. "How the fuck could you?"

"How could I do what?" Marco was completely confused.

"I thought all this time you'd done what you'd done because Samson was watching. That you had to play a part to get us to safety. Not that you think so little of me you could fuck me while I was practically unconscious."

"No," Marco shook his head almost frantically. "I...the omega juice—"

"Makes me horny as fuck and begging for it. I've had it before and survived every time."

"But—" Then Marco understood. He thought...bile rose and threatened to overwhelm him. Kai thought Marco had taken advantage of him. *Because I could.* Marco stared at Kai in absolute horror. Kai took one more look that screamed betrayal and went into the bathroom. He didn't need to be a shifter to hear the click of the lock.

Marco turned blindly and raced through the connecting door and out to the kitchen. He pushed past Chrissy, not even hearing what she tried to say. He had shifted into his cat before he'd gotten to the bottom of the stairs and ran outside. Maybe he should never come back.

Chapter Nine

Kai leaned his head on the shower wall, glad the sound of the water drowned out his sobs. He didn't understand. How could Marco do that? How could he humiliate him so much? What had changed in the man who had refused to touch him for fear of putting him in danger to... Kai shook his head. It made no sense. Wasn't this exactly what he was afraid of though? How many times had he trusted the wrong person?

He'd been sixteen the first time he'd been sold. He hadn't even been sold to an alpha that time. Maeve owned some holiday lets. Used to rent them to humans so she needed someone who couldn't shift. At least she hadn't wanted to fuck him, just have free labor, or free to her, and she daren't use illegals. Him she could pass off as a family friend. If anyone asked, his parents would insist he was supposed be there. He remembered Maeve telling him how much she had paid for him after he worked his first sixteen-hour day. A hundred dollars. A hundred *fucking* dollars. That was all he was worth.

But it hadn't been all miserable. There had been another boy. A wolf shifter from San Antonio. Adam would never say why he was there, but they'd become friends then fooled around a little. A year later Maeve asked if Kai and Adam wanted to make some money. Some real cash. They'd said yes of course because they both knew the chances of getting away without any money was less than zero.

It had been a party. Kai had never questioned what the men had given them to drink. They'd both just assumed it had been human alcohol, but it wasn't and it had brought on Kai's first heat pretty fast. He didn't remember how many humans had fucked him that night, but he remembered thinking it was ironic that they had used condoms to make sure they didn't catch anything from him, not that they could get him pregnant obviously.

But what was so much worse was that the second time he was asked he had agreed. Maeve had paid the money she'd promised and it had seemed the only thing he could do to have any hope of a future. When she'd sold him, they'd ripped him out of his room before he'd had chance to get to where his cash was stashed so it had all been pointless.

Then he'd been convinced he was in love. His alpha had apologized for the way his enforcers had taken him. Told him he would look after Kai and that he never had to worry. Kai scoffed, turned the shower off and immediately heard Chrissy's voice cooing softly to Maddox and his heart thudded. *I know her.* He did, but he didn't even wait to get dry just dragged a towel around his waist and burst out of the bathroom. Chrissy blew a raspberry on Maddox's belly and he giggled. She looked up and smiled. "He's all changed. Dinah sent me to say breakfast was ready."

Kai stumbled over to the bed and scooped Maddox up, his pulse thundering in his ears. "How did you get in?" His bedroom door was locked.

Chrissy eyed him carefully then just gestured to the corner. He followed her glance over at the door to Marco's room and saw it was ajar. He also knew instantly Marco wasn't in there. "Let me take him while you get dry."

Kai just stopped the word "no" leaving his lips, but the silence was uncomfortable and he tried to cover it by perching on the edge of the bed. He didn't put Maddox down though. He knew Chrissy wouldn't hurt Maddox. He knew it, but his brain seemed to be on a constant loop of Maddox being ripped away from him.

She smiled gently and stood. "Breakfast's ready. Don't forget." Then she walked over to the connecting door and left, closing it behind her. Kai sat on the bed and tried to stop shaking. After a moment he stood and laid Maddox in the crib and went for another towel from the bathroom.

He rubbed himself dry wishing it was Marco doing it. He came to a standstill, conviction that he had made a huge mistake washing over him. What have I done? What had he been thinking? This was *Marco*. The man who had risked his own life for him and Maddox. Twice. He had gone into the challenge prepared to die. Kai covered his mouth to halt the next sob. He almost couldn't blame him, but it made no sense. Why would Marco fuck him if Samson hadn't been there? They had to talk. But he'd just told Marco he didn't trust him. Even before that he had refused the bite. And he'd seen the hurt and horrified look on Marco's face before he left.

All the way home he'd begun to think he was starting to love Marco and believe that they were mates, but he'd been wrong before. Had he mixed up kindness for love again? How did he trust himself? How did he know this wasn't the same?

The fact that Chrissy didn't mention Marco was significant, especially as her shifter sense of smell would tell her exactly what they had been doing last night. Kai grabbed some clothes for Maddox and dressed him. He looked so cute in his red pants and matching striped tee. There was even a little cardigan to go with it. Kai added a pair of socks and Maddox was ready.

He wasn't, and it wouldn't make a difference what he wore.

Kai pulled on the first pair of jeans his fingers closed over and added a plain black tee. He didn't bother with shoes or socks. He picked up Maddox, his baby scent immediately calming Kai's nerves.

He looked at the bedroom door and then, since his legs were shaking, he sat down again. He hoped Marco was in the kitchen, it just seemed an awfully long way away. He also wished Chrissy hadn't gone, but he and Marco couldn't talk in front of an audience even if Marco would listen. There was a soft knock at the door. "Kai? It's me, Emmett. Can I come in?"

He whooshed out a breath and he opened the door. Emmett was on his own. "Where's Josie?"

Emmett chuckled and hugged both Kai and Maddox. "In the kitchen being fussed over by Nana." He steered Kai out of the room and kept up the chatter until they got to the bright, sunny kitchen.

Marco wasn't there and Kai's heart dropped to his bare feet. Dinah, Chrissy and Ryker were there. Calvin sat in the corner tucking into some toast and waved as soon as he saw Kai. Ryker and Chrissy both smiled and left. Emmett led him over to the corner where a couple of hammock-type baby chairs had been set up. Dinah passed Josie to Emmett and then turned to admire Maddox. She never asked to hold him though, which relieved Kai a little.

"I hope you boys are hungry," she said archly.

Emmett patted his belly. "I can't wait for real food."

Kai eyed him. "Just be careful for a couple of days. It takes a week or so for things to get back to normal." Emmett strapped Josie in one of the chairs and sat down. Kai thought about it, but kept ahold of Maddox. "She's gorgeous."

"Right back at you." Emmett grinned. "So, tell me all about it." Kai opened his mouth to tell Emmett a really cute story about his birth then closed it because it would have been a lie.

"Shaun was nice. He didn't rush me or ask for sex before Maddox was born or even after. Maddox was born about three weeks after I got there. There were seven kids in total. No school or clinic because the pack was so small, but Shaun tried. *Was* trying."

"Why didn't you call me?" Emmett asked.

Kai pressed his lips together. "Because I was lonely," he whispered. "I wanted to come back here."

Emmett shuffled over and put his arm around Kai and Kai leaned in. "I felt so stupid. Nearly as soon as I left I regretted it, but I couldn't keep changing my mind." He huffed. "I decided to go cold turkey. I just associated Marco with you and couldn't bear the thought of seeing him and not being able to be with him." Because he knew eventually Marco would say yes to another omega and it would kill Kai.

Emmett squeezed him again and it felt good. "You're here now and that's all that matters. So, birth?"

"He's seven weeks old tomorrow," Kai said proudly. "It was an easy birth which was just as well because it was nearly all over before the pack mother came in to see if I was okay. What about you?"

Emmett's eyes narrowed. "Easy birth?"

Kai nodded defiantly but could feel his mask slipping.

"And you were on your own?" Emmett blurred in Kai's vision. He put a comforting arm around him. "I'd have been terrified."

He had been. It had hurt, and he'd missed his pack so much then that if he could have walked he would have gone then and there. He thought he was going to split in two. There wasn't anyone there to so much as hold his hand. "Tell me why I heard Marco call Fox a wannabe midwife?" He needed distracting.

Emmett grinned and told him the story of his naked midwife and Kai laughed weakly, feeling a little better and maybe even a little hungry. Kai looked up and nearly groaned at the delicious smell as Dinah came forward with pancakes and bacon. She put them down on the table and went back for their juice. Kai still hadn't plucked up enough courage to put Maddox down when Emmett patted the seat next to him. Dinah looked at Kai. "I don't want to interrupt. I need to get my pies in the oven."

Taking what little courage he had by the scruff of the neck, Kai held out Maddox. "I think Maddox needs to meet his Nana."

Dinah's smile was worth it. She sat down and took Maddox. "We'll stay right here," she pronounced and Kai relaxed enough to eat.

Calvin sidled up to Emmett and Kai glanced over seeing another little boy and an omega he didn't know. "Can I go play with Joshua?" Emmett looked up and waved at the omega who waved back. Emmett kissed Calvin.

"For an hour before school." Calvin grumbled good-naturedly and ran off with his friend.

"School?"

Emmett filled Kai in on all the new additions to the pack. "Marco has a proper clinic now," he added. Kai put his fork down, his appetite deserting him at the first mention of Marco. Maddox had gone to sleep in Dinah's arms and she was humming softly to him. "I am available for all babysitting duties." She waggled her eyebrows. Kai laughed along with Emmett, but the thought of voluntarily leaving Maddox with someone else made his breakfast threaten to reappear.

"So, am I ever going to find out what happened with the challenge?" Emmett patted Kai's arm.

Kai looked up at Emmett not knowing where to start. "I think I screwed up," he blurted out.

"I can go," Dinah said handing Maddox back to Kai, but Kai shook his head. He hadn't known Nana, as all the omegas called her, long, but she had been really kind and he trusted her. He kissed his sleeping son and told them both as much as he could remember from when the auction started.

Emmett glanced at Dinah. "Do you know what they gave him?"

She nodded and then bent and scooped up Josie who was nearest to her as if she needed the comfort of a baby to hold. Maddox was out like a light. "You were given concentrated omega juice. The new sort."

Kai frowned. "But I've had it before. To be honest I just thought they gave me too much." He was sure he vaguely remembered Charles saying that to Samson.

"Chrissy told me about the new stuff," Dinah explained. "It used to be a mix of GHB and animal sedatives, but this is laced with something similar to Viagra. It's a dangerous cocktail." Emmett gasped and Kai felt the color drain from his face. "Two omegas over in Atlanta recently died from it."

"That's awful," Emmett said and glanced in shock at Kai. Kai tried to take it in.

"It makes sense though. Before it just made me horny and stupid. Even with the GHB I remembered mostly what happened. Marco said I was nearly unconscious at the end."

Dinah pursed her lips. "It's very dangerous. Muscle cramps can eventually lead to seizures. You could have suffered a stroke. Very easily died."

"Is there something they can give them to counteract it?" Emmett asked.

Dinah shook her head. "Bluntly?" They both nodded. "The only thing that will relieve it is the omega orgasming. That's what makes it so dangerous. The regular stuff you can just sleep off. With this, an unscrupulous bastard can edge an omega all night. It works for up to twelve hours so long as the orgasm doesn't happen. That's what killed the two omegas in Atlanta. The bastards let themselves get off but kept the omegas on edge until it killed them."

Kai's hand flew to his lips as nausea flooded his mouth. The things he'd said to Marco when all along Marco had been trying to save his life. Kai groaned.

"What is it?" Emmett asked. "You're here, safe. I'm sure Marco will have made sure you were okay."

Kai shook his head mutely, tears threatening. "I have to find him. Where is he?"

"He shifted and went for a run," Dinah said. "That's why Chrissy went to see if you were okay because he charged past her like the hounds of hell were after him."

"I messed up," Kai admitted. "So bad."

Emmett leaned forward. "He'll be back. I advise make-up sex."

Dinah snorted and patted Kai's hand. "We all make mistakes. My son doesn't even talk to me. I have three grandbabies I've never even seen."

Kai stared in surprise. "But you're wonderful."

Dinah smiled sadly and stood up. "I'm going to get the pies in." She passed Josie to Emmett.

"I think it'll be a while until Marco gets back," Emmett said. "I guess it depends on what you want to do."

But what Kai wanted to do and what he could actually bring himself to do were two different things.

Marco stretched out on his favorite rock, his head on his paws. He'd run off his anger, but he couldn't chase away the hurt. How could Kai think that of him? Marco blew a breath out. But was that really fair? They'd only known each other a matter of weeks and while the mating urge often happened immediately, they hadn't been in any sort of normal scenario before or since to have the chance for Kai to get to know him.

66

And he hadn't stuck around and tried to explain. He caught a scent of something familiar and shifted back, sitting up, knowing his alpha was expecting communication skills better than a roar. The early morning sun warming his skin was enough and he turned to see the black wolf pad out of the forest. When he sat down though Ryker was human. "Wanna tell me why your mate looks like his world has ended and you're out here on your own?"

Marco chuffed, his panther form still close to his skin even though it wasn't visible. "I don't know where to start, but he's not my mate."

"I've got time," Ryker said and fell silent. Marco told him what had happened.

"He thinks—" Marco swallowed around the tightness in his throat. "He thinks I used him."

Ryker winced. "But that's easily explained and I'm guessing since he's with Dinah and Emmett that won't take long to straighten out. What I wanted to discuss is his health."

"There doesn't seem to be any immediate physical problems. I want to get a full workup done when he's talking to me."

"I actually didn't mean that." Ryker told him the reaction he'd had to Chrissy.

Marco slumped. "I'm not surprised he has some form of PTSD. I saw some of it, but I didn't stick around to see him with anyone else." He was so fucking useless. "Some medic I am."

"You're an excellent medic and you do exactly what you're trained for. You just aren't a therapist. I had a similar problem with Emmett and then Calvin. Any other child would have gone to talk to a professional counselor but obviously with shifters it's not that simple. Even with all Zeke's contacts he hasn't found anyone yet. They have them for the charity, but they're strictly human and no one we're ready to trust as of now."

"What did you do about Calvin?"

"Gave him security. Kept him with his alpha. He still worries and we haven't attempted to take him off site yet, but we're planning a trip to Asheville soon."

Marco bit back the first answer he wanted to give. The thought of

Ryker sticking close to Kai made him want to hit something. He hadn't ever considered himself possessive or jealous like he knew the wolves got, but he was clearly wrong. "What exactly are you suggesting?" he tried and failed to keep the frostiness out of his voice.

Ryker chuckled. "Marco, you're as much of an alpha as I am. Just because you choose to submit to me doesn't mean you can't help Kai." Marco relaxed a little. "Besides which, if I were to try it, it would probably make things worse with Kai at the moment. Being an omega is warring with his fear. He's touch starved. Shifters need the closeness of their mate or their alpha and in omegas that's increased a hundred-fold. But he's scared. He needs you, but he's wary." Ryker leaned forward. "He needs to know you're dependable. That he can trust you, not just with him, but with Maddox. Give him security with no sex to complicate things." Ryker paused. "From what I know of him it might not be just that. The person Kai might not trust is himself, and as a shifter, not trusting his own instincts will be messing with his psyche on a very deep level."

Marco stood, and for a moment missed his dad so much he physically ached. His dad had been a quiet soul. Loved nothing more than books. The high point of his day was the crossword. His parents weren't true mates and didn't live together, which was probably good because his mother would have driven his dad into an early grave. He missed his dad and brothers, but he had accepted he wouldn't ever see them again. His dad would have liked Kai and he would have adored Maddox.

Ryker smiled as if he'd said all that out loud. "I'm going to sit here for a bit." Marco shot his alpha a grateful glance, shifted, and ran all the way back to the pack house. He approached the pack house from the side, fully shifted back, and found a neatly folded pile of clothes on one of the steps. He hadn't let the omegas here see his cat because he hadn't wanted to frighten them. His cat weighed in at 550lbs, larger even than the non-shifters. He'd seen the Panthera's claw and he was bigger than every one of them. First born cubs often were, and that coupled with being the Panthera's son made him huge even if she wasn't. Another reason why he hated his mother. She'd expected him to be her personal bodyguard.

Trotted him out for council functions and he was always expected to be in his animal form to look impressive.

It had taken seven cats to take him down when James had been murdered and he'd only finally allowed it because he thought if he surrendered it would save James's life. He'd been so wrong.

Chapter Ten

Kai's heart was ready to stop by the time Marco finally returned. Despite what Emmett and Dinah had insisted, he was convinced he would never see him again and was nearly shaking with relief when Marco let himself into the pack house.

Marco didn't look at him though, just continued up to his room. After a moment, Kai followed to his own room and put a sleeping Maddox in his crib. He walked to the adjoining door and after knocking once, opened it. Marco was sitting on his bed.

"I'm sorry."

Marco turned to look at him. "You have nothing to be sorry about."

"I didn't know though." He wanted Marco to understand. "I didn't realize it was different. Dinah told us."

Marco nodded but he seemed defeated. "I should have hung around to explain."

"And I should have trusted you," Kai said and took a step away from the door.

"Why?" Marco asked quietly. "You didn't have any reason to trust me."

"Apart from the fact you were willing to give your life for me?" Kai's heart thumped.

"As would a lot of people here," Marco pointed out. "Ryker for one."

"I'm a mess," Kai admitted. "I'm not surprised you don't want me."

Marco looked at him, incredulity stark on his face. "Not *want* you? Sweetheart, I've wanted you since the second I first saw you."

Kai's breath came out on a sob and Marco stood. In a second Kai was in his arms. Marco hushed him and held him tight. "This is what we're going to do. We're going to take things slow. We're going to wait until you're comfortable—"

"I am," Kai wailed. "I was an idiot."

Marco stepped back. "Okay. Then go get Maddox and give him to me. You go visit with Emmett." Kai's immediate fear must have shown on his face, but Marco's resigned smile was gentle. He dropped a kiss on Kai's forehead. "See what I mean? You need to trust me and I'm quite happy to wait until that happens."

"But I don't want to wait," Kai whimpered.

Marco sighed. "And I don't want you to doubt yourself or change your mind. Neither of us could go through that again. We need to take it slow."

Five days later Kai rolled over in his empty bed and put his hand on the now cold indent on the pillow next to him. A wail from Maddox registered, that had obviously woken him up. Every night, Marco had held him in his arms until Kai went to sleep, but by the time he woke up Marco had gone back to his room, sometimes left their rooms altogether. Kai understood why Marco had insisted on doing things this way, but instead of getting to know each other he felt like their relationship was on a knife's edge. He'd tiptoed around his mate so much his toes hurt and he knew Marco was doing exactly the same.

It didn't help that Maddox had gone from being the most chill baby ever to being the crankiest. Kai even thought he'd jinxed it because of him sympathizing with Emmett over Josie keeping them awake and being secretly glad Maddox had never been a problem. But the night after Marco had gone to his own room, it had started. Not that if Marco was in his room he ignored them, he always came the moment he heard Maddox start to cry. But a few times Kai had sent him away and told him to shut the door so he could get some sleep. Kai could nap during the day, but Marco was busy in the clinic and could not. Along with his normal duties, Marco was also worried about Darriel who seemed increasingly unwell. Consequently, Kai barely saw him.

An hour later Kai hushed Maddox as much as he was able, but nothing was working. He wasn't too surprised when Marco opened the connecting door. He held out a hand to Kai. "Let's go for a walk."

Kai gaped. It was one a.m. Marco lifted an eyebrow, but kept his arm steady until Kai tucked Maddox into the sling and clasped Marco's hand. Marco grabbed a blanket and a bottle of water. Maddox had just been fed, so there was no need to bring milk.

They stepped outside into the warmth of the September night. Their rooms didn't have balconies, but that was okay. There was a small area to the side of the main steps where the pups played, Marco led Kai there. He spread the blanket out and reached into the sling and held Maddox while Kai sat down. Kai raised his face to the breeze and caught the faint scent of clematis. Marco passed the baby to Kai and stepped back, stripping quickly. "Don't be frightened."

And he shifted. Just like that. Kai was too stunned to have the chance to object even if he was going to. Marco was beautiful. The one time Kai had seen him before he'd been too upset to appreciate it. He should be scared he supposed. A huge, very powerful predator was currently laying on its belly and sniffing Maddox's toes. Kai took a moment to remind himself this was Marco because his cat's head was bigger than Maddox. Maddox who had been whimpering and grousing on and off for hours fell totally silent and just stared at the huge animal in front of him. Kai knew human babies could only see up to around twelve inches at this age, but shifter sight was a little better and he seemed totally enraptured. Marco shuffled a little closer as Maddox held out one chubby fist. Kai held his breath, heart hammering as the giant panther moved within touching distance. He desperately wanted to snatch Maddox back, but this was *Marco*. Marco who had been willing to die for them. Marco who wanted Kai to trust him.

Maddox reached for the panther just as Marco snuffled the baby and

Maddox let out a shriek that made Kai jump. Then Maddox batted Marco's head and Marco shuffled nearer until his huge head lay next to Kai's thigh. Maddox loved it. He bounced and kicked and cooed with excitement, especially when he got ahold of Marco's ear and tugged. Even Kai laughed a little weakly at that. Marco nudged Maddox's foot with his nose and Maddox cooed and smiled. It was adorable. Well, cute now that Kai was assured the huge panther wasn't going to eat his son as a late-night snack. Maddox investigated as much of Marco as he could reach. He was especially fond of his ears and kept trying to grab them. Marco shoved his nose in Kai's belly and Kai chuckled and scratched behind the ear Maddox wasn't abusing. Another moment and Kai realized that Maddox's eyes were finally closing, and his little fist relaxed. Marco kept his huge head under Maddox's hand as he drifted off to sleep. When they were both certain he was out for the count, Marco shifted back, dressed, and they walked quietly back to their rooms. Marco got Maddox settled while Kai went to the bathroom, then curled up in bed. He desperately wanted Marco to stay, but fully expected him to go back to his room. "Hold me while I go to sleep?"

Marco slipped between the sheets and Kai smiled happily. Marco rolled over onto his side, reached out with his arm and hauled Kai close to him, turning him over and tucking his back to Marco's chest. Kai wriggled delightedly.

"Go to sleep," Marco whispered. Kai tried to judge from the tone of his voice if Marco was angry, but he didn't think so. He could be wrong of course. That seemed to happen with alarming regularity.

Marco propped himself up on his elbow and gazed at Kai. "Tell me what that thought was."

Kai's heart jumped in his chest. What did Marco mean? "Which thought? I didn't say anything." Was he sick of Kai trying to get his act together?

"I felt you suddenly tense when I told you to go to sleep."

Kai bit his lip. "I thought you might be angry with me."

"But you weren't sure?" Marco asked gently, very gently. Kai didn't reply, but he didn't think he had to. Marco seemed able to read him like a book. "I think after what you've been through you don't trust your

73

emotions. You're terrified you're going to confuse being treated decently with love."

Kai was stunned. Marco's guess was spot on. "All shifters' senses are pretty accurate, whether you can change into a wolf or not. You just don't believe what your body is telling you."

"I'm scared you're going to get fed up with me."

"Never," Marco said firmly. "I think we're both just waiting for something to go wrong. *Expecting* something to go wrong." He glanced over at the crib. "I think that's what's upsetting Maddox."

Kai frowned. Huh? He was so full of relief that Marco seemed to understand him it took his brain a second to catch up.

"He's picking up on us, our stress. Shifter babies are tuned into the needs of their pack. It's instinctual, even if obviously it's not an actual conscious thought. He can sense our worry and he's reacting to that the only way he knows how."

"That makes sense," Kai admitted. "So, what are we going to do about it?"

"I think we need to talk. *Really* talk." Marco kissed Kai's neck patiently while Kai valiantly tried to get his scattered thoughts together. "I'll go first," he said in gentle amusement. He took a steadying breath. "You crept up on me. I wasn't ever going to have a mate because you know how much that mate would be in danger. The fact that I'm a panther shifter is now the worst kept secret ever. The squad knew obviously, but I never shifted where any of the omegas here could see me. I didn't want to shine a light on where I was. I changed my human last name to Bastien after a science fiction author I love, but my pack name is Stanza. Marco is my real first name. I decided it was common enough. And to be honest, I'm pretty sure the Panthera knows exactly where I am but as long as I don't make waves for her it would be more awkward if I was dead."

"You said you have a brother?" Kai asked hesitantly.

"Two. Both younger. Nathaniel and Nicholas. Twins. Nicholas got me out after my last beating."

"Do you think she would have let you die?"

"Then? Yes. That was nearly fifteen years ago. Now? I'm honestly not sure. I'm thirty-four and probably way too old for you," he said with a grin because shifters didn't care about that. "I've reached out to Emmett's grandmother and I'm hoping she'll be able to come here. She's doing some investigating of her own first which is why the delay, but the pack is secure so you don't need to worry." He accompanied the words with a soft kiss that made Kai's toes curl. "Now, your turn."

"I was the middle one of three. I have an older brother and a younger sister. Dad was a beta. We didn't have a lot of money and the pack was poor, but I was happy until it became obvious that I wasn't going to shift. At the same time the alpha died and his uncle took over." Kai closed his eyes briefly and felt Marco's arm tighten around his waist. He took a steadying breath. "Everything was different. The women were segregated. Even mated pairs no longer ate together. The kids who were over eight and hadn't shifted were herded up one night. We were told we had to run. That we might be killed if the enforcers caught us and thought we hadn't tried."

Marco pressed his head to Kai's. "I'm so sorry sweetheart. An enforced shift. It's barbaric but I've heard of it."

Kai swallowed. "One boy shifted so he was allowed to go back to his mom. Another cut his leg and when the enforcers found him, he'd bled out because he couldn't shift."

"And you?"

"They found me just before dawn. I was taken back to the pack house and kept there permanently. I saw my brother, but I didn't dare speak to him or he to me." Garth had teased him when he'd been younger, but he'd never been deliberately cruel.

"Where is the pack? Maybe Ryker could find your mom and dad?"

Kai shook his head. "One of the enforcers who chased us *was* my dad. I served him meals every day and he didn't even look at me. Just pretended like I didn't exist. Then one morning I was woken up and told I was sold."

Marco made a hurt sound in the back of his throat and turned Kai around. Kai burrowed against his warm chest and clung to the feeling of safety.

"Never again," Marco growled. "You're mine. And I know you don't trust that yet." He kissed the top of Kai's head. "But I'm going to spend every day for the rest of my life convincing you."

It sounded perfect and he knew every word Marco had said made sense, but a little voice in the back of Kai's mind still urged caution. Marco's hand rubbed Kai's back through the old T-shirt he slept in. It was nice, soothing. He inhaled the scent of Marco's bare skin and nuzzled closer. They were facing each other. He knew it was biology, but awareness of what he could feel, how close they were pressing, sizzled along Kai's veins like a wildfire. He felt Marco's cock swell against his belly and Marco hummed a little. "Sorry."

Sorry? And another little bit of understanding clicked into place. Their first joining had been instinctual. But now that Marco had thought about what had happened and how Kai had reacted, he didn't want to put Kai in the position of feeling like he was being forced.

"I loved what we did the other night. I know our instincts took over and while that is unlikely to have happened with humans, I knew who was touching me, tasting me. I wanted it, wanted you, and I'm not confused about that." He took a breath. "The thought of Maddox being out of my sight gives me hives. I have to force myself to let Dinah cuddle him, but it was easier with you. I'm just—" He was just what? "Scared. I can't risk Maddox."

"Because of the trauma you've been through." Marco paused. "I'm only a medic, but I think a therapist would tell you that's a perfectly normal reaction. I think you need to tell yourself that. Give yourself a chance to process everything."

Kai knew Marco was right. He pressed his lips against Marco's throat and kissed him.

Marco hummed, lowered his head and took Kai's lips in a sweet kiss that quickly became more until he broke off. "Please," Kai whispered. "Please touch me." Kai moaned and pressed his body closer as every cell in him caught fire. Marco licked and nibbled Kai's throat, then flipped him onto his back, pulling Kai's T-shirt off. Kai watched as Marco took him in. His gorgeous gray eyes just before he closed them and bent his head, taking first one nipple and teasing it to rigidity that made Kai gasp and tremble, then the second. He followed that with hands grasping Kai's sweats and easing them down. Every bare patch of skin got attention from Marco's lips, tongue or teeth until Kai was helpless not to whisper entreaties. To try and thrust his hips in wordless begging.

"What do you need?" Marco's voice came out deeper and more growly than Kai had heard before.

"You," Kai moaned, surprised he was capable of speech. Marco drew Kai's legs up until his knees were bent, all the time keeping his gaze fastened on him.

"Then trust me to give you pleasure."

Kai might have whimpered but luckily Marco didn't seem to need any direction. Kai's cock thickened and Marco rumbled approvingly letting his eyes roam over his naked body before bending and taking Kai's length in his mouth.

Kai gasped in stunned wonder and Marco's eyes met his. The sight of his cock disappearing between those gorgeous lips completely blew his mind. He gripped the sheet he was laying on desperate to claw back some control. His lips parted to say something, but Marco pushed the tip of his tongue inside Kai's slit and the only sound he was capable of was a gasp as the air was forced from his lungs.

Marco let Kai's rigid cock slip from his mouth and grinned. Then he lowered his head and pushed his hands under Kai's ass, kneading each cheek with his large hands and clever fingers.

"I. You." Kai couldn't get his brain to work out what words he should be saying.

"Let go," Marco whispered. "I won't hurt you." Then he bent his head again and swallowed Kai down. It was too much. Too amazing. Too everything. His cock throbbed once in warning as Marco sucked, then Kai squeezed his eyes shut as the world went white and his orgasm hit like a freight train. Marco gentled and moved back up, reaching for him. And somewhere between that moment and the next, he fell asleep wrapped tightly in Marco's arms.

· · ·

"Stop looking at me." Kai blushed fiercely as Emmett sent him a knowing smile the next morning. Marco had woken up Kai with a kiss and handed him a snuggly baby who had been changed and fed while Kai still slept. Marco had to go to the clinic, but he promised to meet them for lunch.

And he'd stayed with Kai all night.

Kai had Maddox in the sling, still loving the feeling of constantly touching him. Emmett was even interested in trying one and had one on order. They were going to share breakfast with Darriel this morning as Kai hadn't seen him since he got back.

"He's depressed," Emmett said quietly as they walked towards Darriel's room. Jack, one of the teenagers, was following them with a loaded tray but since he had his ear buds in constantly they weren't worried about what he might hear.

"Is your dad still visiting?"

Emmett shook his head. "Dad wouldn't tell me, but I think they had a falling out. Not sure about what because I didn't like to ask, but dad flew to Oregon about a land deal last week and I understand he's going to be away at least another one." Darriel looked up and smiled as they entered. Jack put the tray on the dresser then sauntered back out smiling.

"Kai," Darriel greeted him shyly. "I heard you were—" he stopped as he saw the baby sling and utter wonder lightened his face. "Oh, that's Maddox." It wasn't a question and Kai surprised himself by carefully peeling Maddox out of the sling and handing him over. Okay, so he sat next to the bed, but still.

Tears sprang to Darriel's eyes as he reverently held Maddox. "He's beautiful."

Kai chuckled. "I agree, but I'm kind of biased."

"And I'm kind of starving," Emmett butted in, setting Josie's baby seat on the floor next to his chair and started unpacking Dinah's homemade blueberry muffins and lemon scones. Darriel groaned and patted his rounded belly.

"Are they Dinah's?"

Emmett waggled his eyebrows. Darriel kissed Maddox on the forehead and Kai scooped him back up and settled him back in the sling, his heart rate returning to normal. "Has she just gone to sleep?" Darriel asked eagerly, obviously wanting a cuddle from Josie as well.

"She'll be ready for a feeding soon and she's all yours," Emmett promised and Darriel smiled happily accepting the milk and the muffin.

"How are you?" Kai asked.

Darriel swallowed and blew out a frustrated breath. "Marco's worried. I know he is, but he's trying to put a positive spin on it. Every few days I've been spotting a little, and I've still got three weeks or so to get through." Kai clasped Darriel's hand in support. "And I'm so bored," he whispered.

"Well, we're here now," Kai promised. "So, get used to me being here every day." He tilted his head. "Unless Zeke is here obviously."

Darriel flushed and glanced at Emmett awkwardly.

Emmett took his other hand. "This is between us. We are the official OC."

Kai eyed Emmett. "OC?"

"Omega Club," he said and grinned. "What happens at Omega Club stays at Omega Club."

Kai chuckled. "Good one."

Emmett nodded solemnly. "So, dish. What happened?"

"He's human."

"I noticed." Emmett grinned. "And?"

"Not gay."

Kai winced. Wolves were very fluid in their sexuality because they didn't know who their mates would be, but there were some who had definite preferences. He should know.

"He's been lovely, don't get me wrong."

"But?" Emmett prodded.

"But." Darriel sighed. "He treats me like I'm a child almost, and I want more from him."

"And you don't think that's ever going to happen?" Kai asked.

Darriel shook his head. "He'll always be in love with your mom, Emmett, and I can't compete with that if even I wanted to."

"I'm sorry," Emmett said quietly. "I don't know what to say."

Darriel smiled. "What you're going to say is 'My baby needs a cuddle and a bottle, and I need you to do it.'"

Emmett grinned and accepted the change of subject. Darriel fed Josie and Emmett had another muffin declaring Darriel could take the night shift if he wanted. Kai shared as much as he could as well. He trusted these two.

"Where's Harker now?"

"Gran took him," Emmett said. "He's being held by the claw while the council decides what to do."

Kai's eyes widened. "He's still alive?"

Emmett gazed at him. "I'm still new to this. He shouldn't be?" Kai whooshed a breath out. All his worries hitting him with full force. He hadn't given him a thought. He'd just assumed Regina had handled it.

"It's unusual, definitely," Darriel said. "Human jails certainly can't hold shifters, and as far as I know there isn't such a thing for shifters."

"So, what do they do for punishment then?" Emmett asked. "They can't just let him go." Kai and Darriel looked at each other. "Oh," Emmett said in understanding. "Someone kills him I'm assuming."

"Usually the pack of the wronged shifter." Kai glanced at Darriel for confirmation. "I assumed the claw would take care of it."

Darriel shrugged. "You might have to ask Marco or Ryker." Kai shivered, glad when Maddox woke up to distract them.

Emmett patted Kai's hand. "It will be fine. You know neither Marco or Ryker will let anything happen to you." Kai nodded. Of course they wouldn't. He was being silly.

But three days later Kai remembered their conversation and wondered what the hell had gone so wrong.

Chapter Eleven

Ryker made the call for Rescue One to get their asses into gear at just past four a.m. and Marco, as their medic, couldn't exactly avoid it. Emmett immediately came over with Josie because Ryker didn't want Emmett and Calvin in the cabin on their own. Not that Calvin was even awake when Ryker moved him onto the air mattress. Marco knew it was a mark of trust that Calvin's wolf hadn't woken him. Josie was asleep in the Moses basket, so Emmett left her with Kai and went to make some hot chocolate.

"What's happened, Marco?" Kai asked softly so as not to wake either baby or Calvin. Marco had slept with him every night and Kai seemed content with just kissing and cuddling. Kai had briefly mentioned Harker, but Marco had just shrugged and said he was leaving him to Regina. He didn't want Kai to know the whole thing was worrying him.

"Human parents are reporting a missing child. The ranger service called us because there were reports of an animal nearby. There's an older brother who swears he saw a 'ginormous' cat this afternoon and his sister wanted to go pet it. He says she didn't, but they're worried she went to find it," Marco explained.

"A cat," Kai repeated sounding doubtful.

"Yeah, and obviously I don't mean a domestic animal. The parents are going insane. The campground is up at Linville Falls. Well run. The family was in a cabin. Mom went to the bathroom and looked in on the kids. Annabel is five and she'd just vanished. Her mom found a small bathroom window open, they think she got out that way."

Marco kissed Kai and murmured apologies for leaving, but he left as soon as he saw Emmett come back into the room with two hot chocolates.

"Cougars are supposed to be extinct locally," Red remarked as they drove away. "Bobcat?"

Ryker nodded. "That's what I'm betting on, but we're just going to do some sniffing around. The wilderness rescue squad has already been mobilized as well as the fire service and park rangers. We just need to make sure a shifter isn't involved."

Chrissy rolled her eyes. "Sure, because we all know you're going to just walk away when you don't smell a shifter."

"That's the problem though. I could smell a panther—any of us could."

"Just not if it's a panther *shifter*," Chrissy agreed. A kid was a kid though. He knew they were all in for a long day.

Ryker showed his ID and luckily they spotted one of their rangers who discreetly pulled them to one side. "We might have a problem. The older brother is nine and he swears up and down the cat was black and the size of his uncle's Great Dane."

Out here? Marco shook his head. "Could he have been mixed up in the dark? How could he tell the color?"

"Because he saw it earlier, before they went to bed. He says, and I quote, 'It looked like we were in Wakanda.'"

"Fuck," Red swore. "That damn film."

"There aren't many kids who don't know what a black panther looks like now, though," the ranger added.

"Do you think it's a shifter?" Red asked.

Marco rubbed his eyes. "Let's not even get into the technical conversation about panthers not actually being a species, but as far as I know the purely animal ones have been extinct locally for a very long time. Having said that, there are absolutely zero panther clans that would bring their cubs anywhere near a human campground. It just doesn't happen."

"Then let's do a search." They were officially independent consultants for the parks service. They got away with it because of the various shifter packs that were in the area, including the shifters who worked for the parks, like Marco had once done himself.

Ryker grinned as TJ rushed over. Their part-time member of Rescue One had been delayed in transferring because his mate had been ill. But they were all set to move in a week and Shauna was better, pregnant with their fourth pup, but better. "Hey, stud," he teased.

TJ rolled his eyes. "About time you assholes got here." But he fell into step with them.

They hiked a little higher than the campground. "Bobcats are nocturnal," Marco remarked. "And normally frightened of humans." He glanced at the others. "I think I should go in on my own and shift."

Ryker heaved a sigh. "I don't like it, but I think you're right." Marco stripped and left his clothes with the team. He agreed that if he caught any kind of scent he would call them as soon as he could shift, unless the scent was the child in which case he had to get to her as quickly as possible. Chrissy affixed a small emergency pack to his back. The pack held a phone, emergency supplies and a pair of shorts. It was also padded so as to hide the smell of what was in there. Marco set off. He picked up an odd scent almost immediately and paused trying to work out what it was. Human definitely, but he couldn't tell how old the scent was. Since the humans hiked this close to the campsite, it would be impossible to differentiate. He padded some more and caught the scent of a black bear, but that was old. He avoided some panicked wild turkeys that didn't like predators his size and headed deeper into the trees. It was so quiet just before dawn he could hear the wild mice scurrying away.

Then he stopped. It was the sound that hit him first more than the scent. Definitely human. He inhaled and caught the scent of a big cat. Not that he could tell what type it was. He just knew something large was too close to the human scent. Marco padded forward silently, his animal naturally quiet. The human scent got stronger until he peered between some trees and stared in astonishment. His heart pounded. It was the child, but she was lying on her side, eyes shut, not moving under a small, tattered blanket. He caught movement out of the corner of his eye and in one move Marco bounded towards the child. He rolled and jumped a fraction too quickly for the cat that tried to bite his jugular, and he was able to put himself between Annabel and the panther.

A very *young* panther. Almost a cub. Not that it meant there weren't more around somewhere. In the wild, panthers were expected to make their own way once they were a year old. The younger panther seemed to sigh and in a moment he was looking at a young girl. "We can't talk unless you shift."

He shifted and stared, then quickly grabbed his pack for the shorts. He doubted if she was older than ten, eleven. She nodded as if confirming something to herself. He heard the noise behind him and registered that Annabel was sitting up and yawning, then he whipped his head back to the shifter, immediately on guard again. She looked awfully familiar, but he didn't know why. The young shifter grinned.

"Hello, brother."

Brother? "You know me?" Marco tried to unscramble his thoughts.

"Katrina. *Trina.*" She pointed to herself. "I know you're Marco, because Nicholas showed me a picture. I saw you a few days ago talking to the wolf. But I didn't dare come anywhere near you with him there."

Marco gaped. She'd seen him with Ryker. "You're my sister?" The human child stood up and toddled over to Trina. She held her hand out and Annabel clutched it. "As soon as I saw you were trying to protect Annabel from me, I knew you were the same panther shifter I saw with the wolf."

"I'm hungry." Annabel interrupted and looked up at Marco hopefully as if he was going to alter that fact. His sister shrugged.

"Do you have any food?"

Marco nodded in a daze and picked his pack up from the ground. He pulled out two space blankets, wrapped the child in one and gave her some water and a protein bar. Trina refused the other blanket and dug out her own small pack from behind the tree and pulled on some clothes. A threadbare, torn pair of sweats and a too large t-shirt. A filthy too large t-shirt. "I have lots of questions, but the first one is why do you have the human child?"

Trina flushed. "I didn't take her," she said quickly, "but I shifted earlier and we spoke. Stupid I guess, especially as she decided to come and find me because she said her brother was being mean. She was lucky she only found me."

"Why are you here? Aren't they missing you? I can arrange a ride home for you."

Trina hissed in a breath. "You can't send me back. She will kill me. Take the child." She started backing away, complete panic in her face.

"Trina, no." Marco soothed. "I'm not going to make you do anything. I want you to come home with me, get some proper food. Meet my friends and family."

She looked wary but hopeful. "You promise not to tell Mother?"

"Absolutely. But I have to separate you two. Annabel's mom is frantic."

"I didn't know how to get her back safely without being seen. I was waiting for her to wake up. I've been shifted to scare off anything else that wanted to come near her." Trina smiled at the little girl who was chugging the water like her life depended on it. He held his hand out to both of them.

"Let's go find my alpha. He'll know what to do."

"Your alpha?" Trina said in confusion. "Is that the wolf you were talking to?"

"I have much to explain." Marco grinned, almost giddy with both the thought of reconnecting with some of his family and relief that Annabel was safe. Because they were in their human forms, the others were able to hear them approach and they met up as they exited the trees. Ryker just raised an imperious eyebrow when he introduced his sister, but Chrissy was amazing and had Trina settled quickly. Marco looked at Red. "Can you take the child?" She'd fallen asleep again, so he was carrying her.

Red grinned. "But you're the hero, buddy."

"We all found her," Marco insisted and gave up his burden. Red and TJ headed down the hill. Ryker, Chrissy, and Trina took the sideways route to the truck with him. Marco and Trina stayed out of sight while Ryker pulled it around. No one was worried what Annabel would say about her adventures. Or rather he should say, no one would believe what the five-year-old would say about her adventures.

Marco was thrilled when Kai and Maddox met them in the pack house kitchen. He clutched them both to him and they stayed silent a moment and just breathed each other in. Maddox protested after a few seconds and they drew back laughing softly. Marco gestured to Trina. "This is my sister, Katrina. Trina, this is my m-*friend* Kai and his son Maddox." Marco had nearly said mate without thinking, but Kai smiled and shyly greeted Trina.

Dinah insisted that no one was allowed to ask or answer any questions until they were all fed and warm, so it was at least another forty minutes until they were all settled. Red still wasn't back but they weren't surprised.

"How old are you?" Marco asked.

"Thirteen. Fourteen next January," Trina said promptly.

"You're twenty years younger than I," he murmured. "The Panthera had no daughters when I left, but I had two brothers."

"And that's important?" Kai asked obviously hearing the catch in Marco's words.

Marco nodded. "If the Panthera doesn't birth a daughter, the title eventually goes to the closest female relative of the next generation when they reach thirty." He expanded. "The title wouldn't pass to my aunt, for example. But if my aunt had a daughter then it would pass to her." He looked at Trina. "But none of that explains why you are here."

"I thought it was twenty-one," Emmett said, frowning.

"We can take over at twenty-one if both the Panthera and heir want that," Trina mumbled over a mouthful of food.

"But they have to take over by thirty," Marco added. "It's really a transition period."

Trina swallowed. "Except none of our line had any girls except me, and the whole clan has none over the age of three."

"Really?" Marco asked in surprise.

"It meant that I would take over in sixteen years if she didn't give

86

permission for the early one." Trina looked at Marco. "And we both know that wouldn't happen."

Marco nodded but explained for Kai. "My mother has tried to campaign to change that rule for a long time."

"Papa told me about you," Trina said. "No one else is allowed to talk about you. It's as if you never existed. Nicholas showed me a picture when I asked, but he was reluctant."

Marco thought that perhaps he should have been upset, but he simply didn't care. He shrugged. "I miss our dad, but I don't give a rat's ass about the rest of them or the politics that go with it."

"It still doesn't explain why you're here," Emmett said gently.

"She was trying to increase the age limit for a Panthera." Trina said. "She wanted the age limit to be dependent upon the age of the Panthera, not the heir. She says the rule is outdated and robs the clan of a Panthera's maturity, and there is a clan on the east coast whose Panthera is in her sixties because she has no direct female descendants and is waiting for the youngest to be of age."

Emmett smirked but didn't say anything.

"But she had you, and thirty isn't immature," Chrissy said, then shot Marco an astounded look as if the same idea had occurred to her.

"What happened?" Marco asked as gently as he could even though sick suspicion roiled in his gut.

"Nicholas started acting weird."

"Nicholas?" Ryker glanced at Marco.

"My younger brother. He was the one who got me out. Weird how?" Marco asked.

"Weird like he wouldn't let me out of his sight."

Marco shot Ryker a worried look. "And what did Mother do?"

"She got angry. Said I wasn't a baby and we both had to stop acting like I was." Marco reached out and squeezed Katrina's hand. "She sent him on a task for the council. Something about a panther being seen with a wolf." Marco nodded. That sounded about right. "But Nicholas was attacked by wolves."

"How do you know?" Marco asked trying to swallow the sick feeling down.

"Because he'd had given me a cell phone. Mother wouldn't let me have one, but Nicholas wanted me to have it for safety. He said if I was ever scared to call him right away." Tears glinted in her eyes and Marco reached over and pulled her to his side. He glanced at Kai who simply took her other hand in his. Maddox was asleep and swaddled in a sling around Kai's chest. Marco knew Trina wouldn't be used to affection from anyone but her immediate family, and probably not even that, but she cuddled into Marco's side.

"What happened?" Marco hardly dare ask.

"Nicholas called me. He'd been ambushed, but the wolves had suddenly run even though there were a lot of them. He told me to hide in a special crawl space until he got back."

"He thought it was a trap." Marco met Kai's gaze.

"I went to the crawl space under the kitchen like Nicholas showed me, but before I could hide three of the claw came into the house. So, I climbed out of the pantry window. Mother had gone out, but there's no way they would have gotten in unless she knew."

Kai tilted his head questioningly.

"She had guards and an alarm," Marco bit out, fury heating his blood. "How long ago?"

"Nine days. I took a bus. I wanted to find you and I needed somewhere to be at least dry while I found out what was happening, but my wallet and phone got stolen while I was asleep, so I couldn't call Nicholas. He has no idea where I am either." *Jesus.* She could have been killed. "I knew you were somewhere here, but not exactly where. I couldn't believe it when I saw you."

"How did you know where I might be?"

Trina glanced down sheepishly. "Mother ignores me most of the time. I suppose I got used to behaving like I was invisible. Papa had come to the house and they were talking. She was angry because he was really excited that he'd found out where you were. That you were a medic for the ranger service up here."

"What did Mother say?" He dreaded to guess.

"She asked him what made him think she didn't already know."

Of course she did.

Her eyes widened as Dinah interrupted them all with another huge plate of sandwiches and cake. She followed that with fresh coffee, juice and cold milk. Trina fell on the food like she was starving and Marco chuckled. Trina was a typical shifter and could probably eat her body weight in food. She would have had very little food in the last nine days, especially as he doubted she was used to hunting for it. Ryker stood and gestured to the door. Marco glanced back at her. "I have to sort out some things for my alpha, but Kai, Emmett and Chrissy are here. Will you be okay? I won't be long."

Trina smiled, sticking her chin up stubbornly. Marco smiled at that.

He went over to the other door with Ryker. Red had finally returned and joined them both. "I hate to say it," Ryker said, glancing at Marco. "But I think we need to call Regina."

"I agree. I'm completely out of my depth on this one. Unless we can prove her negligent, I think my mother has every right to come and take Trina."

"Would Nicholas support you if we went to the council?"

"I honestly don't know. He obviously protected Trina and got me out, but whether he would openly defy her I don't know."

They bedded Trina down in one of the omega rooms just two doors away from them. Marco explained exactly where he was. He gave her a cell phone from Chrissy's stash and made sure she knew how to use it. Ryker had contacted Regina and she was going to visit in the morning.

Kai had been quiet and supportive all day. Marco returned to their rooms just as Kai was lifting Maddox out of the baby bath and wrapping him in a huge towel. Marco leaned on the door frame and watched. Kai was completely besotted with Maddox. He understood, Marco was besotted with both of them. He emptied the water while Kai dried Maddox, diapered and dressed him. Marco got the bottle Kai had prepared and held his arms out. "May I?"

Kai grinned. "That would be perfect actually. I need a shower."

"So, baby," Marco murmured when he heard the shower start and knew Kai wouldn't hear him. "What are we going to do to get your daddy to trust me?" Maddox sucked furiously and Marco chuckled. He smiled as Maddox gazed right at him, watching him for a while. His hazel eyes were unusual for a shifter, but they were exactly the same as Kai's. "Because this is a two-man job, buddy, and I'm going to need your help."

"What is?"

Marco looked up at Kai who was just exiting the bathroom accompanied by clouds of steam. "You could have taken your time. Maddox and I were in no hurry." He looked down to see the little cutie's eyes closing. "I went to check on Darriel earlier. He was thrilled you let him hold Maddox."

Kai sighed. "It's not that I don't know he's safe. In my head I know all that."

"I know," Marco said smoothly and stood. "Here, kiss your son. I'm going to my room to grab a shower." Kai opened his mouth to say something, but he closed it and nodded. Marco held back the sigh. The go slow plan was killing him.

Chapter Twelve

"Hey"

Marco turned the corner on his way to the meeting room and grinned as Emmett's dad put his hand out. "Zeke, good to see you." They shook hands. Marco had gotten used to the human way of greeting. The clan, he thought with amusement, never touched another person without express permission. Even children were taught to wait until their parents instigated it. He liked the human way better, but he really liked the wolf pack way of constantly touching each other.

Especially if it involved him touching a certain omega.

"You joining us?" He tried to keep the surprise from his voice, but he knew Zeke would never forgive clan politics for the death of Emmett's mom. He had been polite but reserved with Regina since she had saved Emmett's life, which the pack was grateful for.

He rolled his eyes. "I can behave." His smile fell. "How's Darriel?"

Marco wasn't surprised at the question and they both walked into the meeting room and helped themselves to the coffee already set out. "Bored. Frustrated. Scared," Marco replied honestly. Zeke winced. Even Marco had thought that Zeke and Darriel's friendship would develop further, but he supposed since Zeke was human he wasn't susceptible to the mating instinct. Apparently he wasn't bi either according to what Kai had told him, so their relationship would always be platonic. But looking at Zeke's drawn and worried expression, Marco wasn't sure. They took their seats as Ryker and Regina walked in followed by Chrissy, who was holding Trina's hand, Red, and Fox. Emmett rushed in a moment later and flung his arms around Regina. Marco watched in astonishment. He'd seen this before, but it still amazed him how she could forgo years of strict upbringing to hug Emmett just as enthusiastically. Her Chanel suit even looked a little hammered from the encounter.

Marco greeted Regina respectfully but warily, smiled and patted the empty seat next to him for his sister who—although cleaned and fed—looked utterly terrified. He reached over and squeezed her hand and Trina didn't let go. *Fine by me.* Regina had swept in with three of her claw and they had stationed themselves at strategic points around the room. Regina smiled at Trina and extended her hand. "It is an honor to meet you Panthera-cub." Marco shouldn't have been surprised at the old name for the Panthera heir. Trina flushed, stood politely, and was brave enough to take Regina's hand. Regina seemed totally calm and collected as usual. "May I call you Katrina?"

Marco had to give Trina props for accepting her full name with a nod, clearly understanding that Regina wasn't going to use nicknames. She sat down, neatly folding her hands in her lap. Marco brushed her shoulder with his in support and she sent him a weak smile.

Regina inclined her head in acknowledgement of Marco then looked at Ryker. "With the obvious exception, the Stanza clan has no other females of the acceptable generation above the age of three years. Elena Stanza has campaigned vigorously for the past ten years to increase the age of Panthera retirement. That it should be the age of the current Panthera that determines the date of succession, not the Panthera-cub." Marco knew this, but he was glad Regina was going over it for everyone else. "Katrina, please tell me what you have told Marco." Trina repeated everything she could think of, including the overheard conversation between her parents and her escape.

Regina glanced at Ryker. "If I were an ambitious woman and going to orchestrate something like this, then time would be of the essence."

"Why especially?" Ryker asked leaning forward.

Regina ticked of the points on her fingers. "One. Katrina is nearly fourteen and could easily claim independence." She shot an amused look at Marco and he nodded in acknowledgement.

"Why is that significant?" Emmett asked.

"Because in clans a fourteen-year-old can declare their majority with the backing of a direct family member," Marco explained.

"You?"

Marco inclined his head.

"And two," Regina continued, "your father has found out where you live and has made it clear he wants to contact you. Both of those factors may induce panic in individuals unfortunate enough to be susceptible to those particular irritating habits." Out of the corner of his eye he saw Ryker try and hide a smile.

"What do you suggest we do?" Marco said in defeat.

"Because if she knows where Marco is, it wouldn't be so much of a stretch to search for Trina in the same place," Red commented.

"Exactly," Regina confirmed and turned to Marco. "I believe the safest place for Katrina is wherever you aren't." She held a hand up at the collective gasps. "And that isn't here either. Elena knows you are here now, so your leaving would be pointless. She would still send her claw to look. We need somewhere safe to put Katrina for the next three months."

"Maybe with Jessie and Seth?" Fox queried. They had a few cabins an hour south which they used for rescued shifters not needing the pack house.

"No," Ryker said immediately before Marco could. "It's simply not secure enough."

"Then where?" Chrissy asked.

"Easy," Zeke said quietly. "Trina comes home with me."

The complete silence at Zeke's pronouncement even took Emmett a moment to break. "That's a really good idea," he said and smiled at his dad.

"But she's a clan member," Marco started hesitantly. Zeke hated the clans, and he didn't blame him.

Zeke focused on Trina and smiled. "I'm Emmett's one hundred percent human dad and along with Ryker I own the organization that runs this place. I have a very secure, luxury penthouse near Asheville and I can move my assistant May in there with Trina."

"May's awesome, and she's a teddy-bear shifter," Emmett added, still smiling. Trina looked startled until Red snorted as he took a sip of coffee, and Zeke chuckled. Marco knew May—even though she was a brown bear shifter—was five feet nothing, if that.

Marco glanced at Zeke. Regina was still silent.

"But more importantly," Zeke said gently. "You will be safe until you turn fourteen and decide what to do."

Trina held his gaze. "Why did Marco seem surprised you would offer?" Marco met Ryker's rueful gaze. Trina wasn't stupid.

"That's my fault," Regina said quietly. "He has no reason to like clan politics."

Trina glanced at Marco for reassurance and he nodded. "I trust Zeke." He hated the thought of her going somewhere else, but he knew Regina was correct. "And I paint a very huge target on you at the moment."

"Security has to be stepped up for you as well," Regina said quietly. "I am assuming you will sponsor Katrina's independence?"

He nodded and shot a worried look at Ryker. "I'm bringing a lot of trouble on your heads. Maybe I should think about distancing myself." But what about Kai? It would kill him.

"No," Ryker and Regina both said simultaneously.

"I will provide extra security," Regina added. "You're safer all in one place." She rose as did all the men and beamed at Emmett. "Now, where's my Josie?"

Zeke stood along with everyone else and said he would put things in motion, that it would take a couple of hours.

Marco blew out a shaky breath. His skin itched. He knew his cat wanted out, that it needed space, but he couldn't shift for a run because he needed to be close in case someone needed him. "Marco?" he glanced at his sister, took in her anxious look and immediately felt guilty, like he was abandoning her.

"I trust Zeke."

"I got that, but I want to ask you something." Marco stiffened, expecting the deserved guilt about to be heaped upon his head. Even Regina could do more than her own damn brother. "Tell me again what my options are. Regina was a little overwhelming."

"Do you want to go outside?"

She nodded and followed him. He spotted two of Regina's claw following them at a discreet distance. He gestured over to the grass where the omegas had been earlier. "We can't leave the grounds."

She followed him and he sat down against a tree. Trina copied him, folding her legs with cat-like grace. "Explain to me about Emmett and his dad?"

Marco told her as much as he knew, and why Zeke would never forgive clan politics for ultimately getting Emmett's mom killed.

"It's never that simple obviously and Regina loved her daughter, but clans never know what to do with members who don't want to fit in." He waved at himself theatrically.

"Am I allowed to like Regina?" Trina said hesitantly.

Marco's eyes widened in astonishment. "Of course." And he understood immediately. Trina was worried about being disloyal. "I actually think she'd be a good person to know. You're going to need help with the clan and Regina is the best person to be in your corner." He then launched into the story of how she rescued Emmett and Calvin by pretending to be a frail old lady and had Trina chuckling by the time he'd finished. He felt guilty he couldn't help Trina as he wished, but he trusted Regina to.

"What do you think Mother will do?" Trina just seemed curious now though, not anxious.

"From what Regina said, I understand it's completely mind-boggling that she's gotten away with you being missing for nearly two weeks, especially with Dad."

Trina raised sad eyes. "Papa was a stranger to me. I saw him a handful of times a year, if that."

"Really?" Marco was stunned. It explained things though.

"It took until I was maybe eight to realize I was a prisoner."

Marco whipped his head around to stare at her. "Go on."

"I thought it was because I was a girl at first," Trina explained. "And younger. That she loved me, so she wanted to protect me." She huffed. "It took me a while—too long really—to work out I was being hidden because she resented me." Marco's heart ached for a different reason this time. "I was eleven, I think, when I realized she wished I'd never been born."

"*What?*" Although why Marco should be surprised, he didn't know.

"I heard her talking. I have no idea to whom, but she was discussing some money-making scheme. I got that it would be a good idea, but then she said what was the point. That the real returns were another twenty years away and why should she do all the work for some other bitch. I understand she meant the 'bitch' was me. Her *daughter*." Marco put his arm around Trina and hugged her close.

"I'm sorry you had to find out so early."

She snuggled into Marco's side. "But if I hadn't, I might be dead." He pressed her to him. He'd never expected to have a family again, and even if Kai was killing him, he could step up for his baby sister.

"You know this is only temporary, don't you? I can move us both somewhere else if you want to leave."

"What about Kai? Even I know mate trumps everything and he has a baby. And I don't mean that in a mean way. Dad used to call it a biological imperative."

Marco sighed. "I don't know what Kai wants. He doesn't trust me, and I'm not sure he wants to be my mate."

Trina scoffed. "I might be too young to be a Panthera but even I know that doesn't come with a get-out clause. What about Maddox?"

"He's not mine." Marco filled her in.

Trina listened until Marco was finished, even though he was judicious with some of the details. "I hadn't realized wolf omegas weren't precious to packs," she finally said with complete honesty.

"And you would think they would be more so," Marco agreed.

"I feel sorry for him, that he won't get the freedom his animal gives him," Trina said. "That must be very hard. I thought for a long time I wouldn't get it either."

"What do you mean?" Marco glanced at her in confusion.

"They thought I wouldn't shift. I think that was why Nicholas was so worried, but I shifted the next day for the first time."

"The next day when?" Marco pressed.

"When I got off the bus after I ran. We were at a rest stop. I don't know how I managed to get myself back together to get back on because it was the longest three days of my entire life. I'd just gotten to Phoenix when I felt it start and that was because this guy was being a dick."

"Trina," Marco muttered in horror and pulled her to him. "I'm so sorry." He should have been there.

"Don't be a dork," Trina chuckled. "You didn't even know I existed."

Which Marco had no comeback for. He nudged her shoulder and let go. "But I do now."

"So," Trina said brightly. "Operation Kai. What shall we do first?"

Marco chuckled despite himself. "I don't know." He didn't. "Let's get your things together. I want to make sure your phone is okay and chat with Zeke and Regina some more." At least he could do this. Operation Trina was coming along nicely, but Operation Kai might fail before it even got a chance to start.

Chapter Thirteen

Kai rolled over and stared at the empty space next to him. It had been two days since Trina had left with Zeke. It had taken a bit to arrange and May needed a few days to alter her schedule, but it was done. He and Marco should have had some time together now, except it didn't seem to be working out like that. Marco had seemed to take forever to shower in his own room last night—as he had done every night—to the point Kai was almost asleep when he had come back. He remembered being pulled into Marco's arms and being hushed, but nothing else. He'd been gone when Maddox had woken up a little after five and Kai had missed him immediately. Kai didn't expect to see him much today either, between his regular clinic duties and the fact one of the other omegas had been threatening to go into labor for the past week.

In fact, he'd barely seen Marco since he'd rescued Trina. Kai was so happy Marco had found his sister, and not for the first time wondered what Garth and Ellie were doing. If they were happy. If they ever thought of him.

He didn't fool himself that his dad ever did. He was probably glad he didn't have to have the constant reminder he had an omega for a son. His mom had been loving when he was younger, but even she had changed when the new alpha had taken over. She'd stopped sticking up for him. He supposed it had been hard and she had Ellie to worry about, but how could parents suddenly stop loving their children because of how they were born? He knew it happened, but it made no sense to him. He would never stop loving Maddox, no matter what.

His belly rumbled a little and Kai tried to remember what he had eaten yesterday. Maybe he was hungry. Maybe he could have a hot chocolate with Emmett? Dinah made it with extra cream. He swallowed quickly, his stomach suddenly not liking that idea. He swallowed again when his stomach *really* didn't like that idea and he just managed to bolt into the bathroom and make it to the toilet before he threw up.

Crap.

Which was his first thought after he'd rinsed his mouth out, but before he'd made it back to bed. Okay, so the likelihood he was pregnant was next to zero. He'd never been sick—morning or otherwise—with Maddox, but he wasn't surprised his belly was acting up. It was stress. He brushed his teeth, went and sat down gingerly on the bed, and reached for the bottle of water there. Maddox was stirring, so he took a couple of sips and decided to forgo a shower until later and just get them both dressed. He was meeting Emmett and Darriel. Darriel wanted desperately to go outside, so Sam, the new beta, had said he would simply carry him.

Thirty minutes later they were both dressed. Kai decided to take Maddox's bottle outside with them, so he grabbed Maddox and all his paraphernalia and headed to the kitchen, already spotting Emmett and Darriel outside. He held his breath a little as he walked through the kitchen, still unsure what had set him off this morning, and strode over to the grass. They had a huge blanket spread out and not surprisingly Darriel was cuddling Josie who was guzzling her milk like it was going out of fashion.

"I'm going to be able to tell what I'm having soon on a scan," Darriel said, the excitement obvious in his voice. Soon Josie had finished her bottle and was asleep. "I can't decide whether to just ask Sarah or not."

"Sarah?" Kai asked getting Maddox's bottle out. "Isn't she one of the kids you rescued from the cave-in?"

Emmett nodded. "Her omega James is thinking of settling in Mills

River. The new alpha isn't anything like the others and James is used to a bigger pack."

"She's a pack mother," Darriel explained.

Kai thought about that. "But so's Dinah."

Emmett shook his head. "No, I don't mean someone like a pack midwife, I mean the traditional sort. The ones who can tell immediately if you're an omega, or if you're pregnant and what the pup's going to be."

Kai's eyes widened. "A pack the size of Mills River would definitely want her then."

Emmett grinned. "Yep, and between you and me, James is a little smitten with the new alpha down there."

Kai grinned. "Really?" They all looked up at the sound of footsteps and Maddox, even though he was on his stomach, raised his head at the sound. "You clever boy," Kai cooed and glanced over as Ryker and Marco approached. Marco smiled hesitantly at him and they both sat down.

"Regina just called. She's put out some feelers to a few people she trusts and Trina still hasn't been publicly acknowledged as missing," Ryker said before kissing Emmett soundly.

"I just can't understand my dad," Marco said, his frustration evident. "We wouldn't call the cops obviously, but the clan should know and be looking. The next Panthera going missing? They should be scouring the country."

"What does Gran suggest?"

Marco glanced at Emmett. "To lie low until her birthday, then Regina can protect her."

"It means there will always be a risk though," Marco said. "It's a long time until she's thirty."

Kai glanced at Marco. "I think we're as safe as we're going to be here." Because they couldn't stop living. Marco met his eyes. He just looked resigned. When he glanced away, Kai's heart squeezed. This was on him. He'd put the defeat in those eyes.

Ryker's phone rang and he stepped away to answer it. After a moment he beckoned Marco to join him. Kai watched them. He hoped that wasn't bad news about Trina. Emmett said something, but Kai didn't hear him. He was watching Ryker and Marco. Ryker had put the phone back in his pocket and they were just staring at each other. His stomach lurched because neither of them was smiling. Kai instinctively reached over for Maddox and lifted him close. "Something's wrong."

They all watched Ryker and Marco as they walked back to them.

"What's happened?" Emmett asked.

Ryker heaved a sigh, but sat and reached for Josie. "We've had a call from the council. They've asked us to take in someone, but before I agree we have to ask Kai."

"Me?" Kai said in astonishment. "Who?"

"Charles," Marco answered.

"No," Kai blurted out immediately. "Absolutely not." Nausea threatened and he breathed out through his nose until it passed.

Ryker nodded. "Fair enough." Kai's heart rate settled when he realized Ryker wasn't going to try and persuade him otherwise.

"But why on earth would they want him to come here?" Emmett asked.

"Because he's an omega," Marco said.

Even Kai was astonished. "I thought he was a gamma."

Ryker shook his head but didn't offer anything else. Kai groaned. "Okay, tell me. Apart from him being an omega, why do they want him to come here, because there are other packs that he could go to."

"Because he's going to need one with a clinic and on-site medical facilities."

Something cold curled inside Kai. "Why?"

"Because," Marco answered, "the enforcers that worked for Samson decided if the boss wasn't there to control them they would have a little fun."

Kai paled. He remembered the enforcer that Charles had stopped going for him. "What did they do?"

"They used him as a fuck toy for three days until he started having seizures, then they dumped him in one of the empty storage units and fled. Eric O'Neal, the alpha from Tallahassee, has taken in some of both Harker's and Samson's wolves and he found Charles when they inspected the place. O'Neal took him home because they have some older omegas, but he got ahold of a knife and threatened to slit his wrists if they didn't let him go. O'Neal sounds like a good guy, but he's out of his depth. The pack can't keep him and no one else seems to know what to do with him. All he will say is that he needs to get back to his alpha. Meaning Samson."

Kai met Emmett's horrified gaze, and pity mixed with resentment. "Will I have to see him?"

"No," Marco said. "We can restrict him until we find somewhere for him to go. Hopefully he won't be here long."

"Okay. Let him come here then." He just couldn't see him. Charles had held his head immobile while Samson had poured that shit down his throat. He would never forgive him for that and him being an omega made it even worse.

Ryker stood and got on his phone. Marco turned to Darriel. "How are you feeling? Ready for your scan in a couple of days?" Darriel nodded eagerly and conversation returned to other things. But Marco didn't look at Kai. He couldn't have made it clearer he was keeping his distance.

Kai hid in his room when the helicopter landed. He knew Fox, Chrissy and Marco had gone to get Charles, but the thought of him being here made his skin crawl. In a lot of ways he'd felt more violated by Charles than Samson. He'd bathed him, and the enema... Kai wrinkled his nose in concentration. He remembered Charles making him have one, but he didn't remember him doing it. In fact, he thought he'd allowed him to go in the bathroom on his own. Kai shrugged defiantly. He had still held him down though. Stared at him and *looked as if he was going to cry.*

Fuck. What if Charles had been as trapped as he was? Kai didn't like that idea. A trickle of shame slithered down his spine because if his experience with Marco had told him anything it was that he seemed to be great at jumping to conclusions. He finished changing Maddox and kissed him when he smiled and kicked his legs. It might have been gas, but it looked like a smile. He picked up Maddox and tucked him into the sling feeling safer almost immediately. Kai liked having Maddox protected in a way that also kept both of his own hands free. He cautiously went into the kitchen. He'd given them enough time to get Charles out of the way.

Ryker was sitting in the corner with his arm around Emmett. Dinah was holding Josie. Kai rushed over. "What's wrong?" His heart started thumping. "Where's Marco?"

Ryker shook his head. "Marco's fine. He's settling Charles. Chrissy is with him."

Kai looked at Emmett who was valiantly trying to stop his tears. "What's the matter?" Emmett just shook his head and looked at Ryker. A quiet conviction swept over Kai. "It's Charles, isn't it?"

Tears rolled down Emmett's face. Kai sat with a whoosh. "Tell me."

"Kai," Ryker started. "None of this is to make you feel bad."

"Tell me."

"He was sold to Samson at fourteen," Ryker said, his jaw clenched so hard it was a wonder he could get the words out.

Kai blanched. He could practically feel the blood drain from his face. "How old is he now?"

"Thirty-nine," Emmett whispered. "He's been with that bastard for nearly twenty-five years." Nausea flooded Kai's system and he swallowed with difficulty.

Kai thought back to what he remembered. "I thought he was older." He'd looked nearer to fifty, not forty. "But why isn't he glad he's free of Samson then?"

"Humans would call it Stockholm syndrome," Dinah murmured.

"And wolves would call it learning to survive," Ryker clipped out.

"Except he doesn't want to live anymore," Emmett whispered and raised teary eyes to Kai. "He begged Marco to let him die if no one is going to let him go back."

Kai didn't know what to say. "He definitely wants to go back to Samson?" It seemed insane to him.

"He says he has no choice. That Samson's his alpha, but he won't say any more," Ryker said.

Kai stood up and without a word left the kitchen. Somehow his feet took him to the clinic without him being conscious of making a decision.

He thought long and hard about the simple act of knocking, but he didn't want to be refused entry, so in the end he simply opened the door and walked inside.

He saw Chrissy first and she practically snarled at him. "Out." He ignored her. Fox just looked like he wanted to punch someone, but he stayed leaning against the wall. Kai met Marco's astonished eyes briefly before his focus returned to the bed. He almost didn't recognize Charles. Gone was the man he remembered from three weeks ago and in his place was a shadow. A dark ghost that was so pale and quiet Kai would have sworn he was a corpse. Except even as his body never moved, his closed eyelids flickered with something. Something haunted. Something so tortured it wasn't even human.

Taking a calming breath in the total silence, he eased Maddox from the sling and hitched a hip onto the cot. He laid Maddox between his hip and the near skeleton lying motionless beside him. Maddox cooed and immediately stuck his legs in the air. Kai lay down and moved closer to Charles trapping Maddox between them. Charles opened blank eyes and stared at Maddox as if he couldn't believe what he was seeing, then a solitary tear rolled down his face. "What...what are you doing?" Charles's voice sounded as broken as the man.

"I'm showing you what you helped save. If you hadn't gotten us out from Samson's, Maddox would have been raised in Harker's pack. Samson was a monster, but Harker was a monster with money and that made him twice as dangerous." Kai stroked a finger down Maddox's cheek. "You saved both of us."

Another tear rolled down Charles's face and he turned his head away as if he couldn't bear to look. Kai glanced at Marco. He was still, listening, and he sent Kai an encouraging look. Chrissy just looked ashen.

Maddox cooed and waved his feet. Kai didn't touch him. He cried out again obviously wanting some attention and for the first time ever, Kai didn't immediately respond. Another beat went by and Maddox screwed his nose up as if he was going to cry, but instead he let out a startled oo-oo noise. Kai bit his lip. Charles turned his head back and looked at Maddox. Maddox waved his fist in the air, then gazed at Charles. Slowly, like it took great effort, Charles raised his hand and extended a trembling finger to the little fist and gently touched Maddox's fingers. Maddox immediately clamped his tiny fingers around Charles's shaky one.

Charles inhaled sharply and more tears leaked out. He lowered his hand until it was resting on the bed, but Maddox didn't let go. He experimented with another couple of oo-oo's, then smiled.

Charles gazed at him as if he couldn't believe what he was seeing. His lips even curved a little as he tried to smile back. It was as shaky and as hesitant as his finger, but it was there. They lay there another moment until Charles's eyes started drooping and Kai got up slowly. "We'll come back and visit you in the morning," he promised. He picked up Maddox and let himself out of the room. He blew out a shaky breath and leaned back against the wall.

The door opened and Chrissy appeared. Silently she wrapped Kai and Maddox up in a hug. "Thank you." Then she went back into the clinic. Kai stood there another moment before he walked back to the kitchen.

Ryker and Emmett were still there. Both looked up warily as he entered. "Where's Charles going to sleep?"

"I suppose one of the omega rooms," Ryker said slowly. "I would need to speak to Marco."

"What about the single room opposite Marco's? It's closer in case Charles needs Marco during the night, but it's still private." It wasn't connecting but it was nearer than the one Trina had vacated. Emmett reached over and clasped Kai's hand.

"Are you sure?"

Kai nodded. *Yes*, he was very sure. He eased Maddox into the sling. "I think we need to go get it ready."

Emmett stood and looked at Ryker. "Can you let Marco know what we're doing?"

Forty minutes later, Kai was surprised when Fox walked into the room cradling Charles as carefully as a newborn, and for probably the first time Kai studied the beta. He was older than both Red and Ryker. Shorter as well, but his well-muscled forearms didn't make him look like he was having any difficulty carrying Charles. He suddenly wondered why Fox wasn't mated. Charles hissed involuntarily when Fox laid him down. Fox shot Marco an agonized look and Kai understood he felt like crap for hurting him, but the man was going to hurt no matter what they did.

Kai pulled up a chair and sat down taking ahold of one of Charles's cold hands. Marco bustled around getting his kit ready and everyone else left. Fox glanced at the bed, then back at Marco. "Text me if you need anything."

Kai smiled at Charles who was awake and watching him. He hadn't tried to take his hand back though. "Why is Fox called Fox?" Kai asked Marco, as much because he knew Charles was listening as he wanted to know. "I mean Red's pretty obvious."

Marco grinned. "Did you know Emmett thought he was a fox shifter?"

Kai chuckled. "I'm not surprised." He looked at Marco. "Is it a secret or something?"

"*Silver* fox," Marco said dryly.

"Ahhh," Kai said. "Yeah, I can see that." Charles closed his eyes again and Kai leaned back when he knew he was asleep. He also knew Maddox would be due a feeding soon. He stood when Chrissy crept in. Marco waved his phone at her. She nodded and sat down as they left the room.

"I texted Chrissy," Marco explained. "To let her know we're keeping someone with him around the clock."

Kai smiled. "That's good."

"He's not eating. *At all*."

"He hasn't been here long though," Kai said.

Marco gazed at him. "He's barely eaten a thing since we got you from Samson's apparently." Kai's eyes widened. "I'm worried this is just another way of him killing himself." Kai put a hand to his mouth and swallowed.

"The reason the enforcers kept him going for three days was because he'd built up such a resistance to the regular stuff. Anyone else would have been dead. And not being able to shift to heal is a huge problem."

"I'll try to stop by as much as I can."

Marco tilted his head and stared at Kai like he was trying to puzzle him out. "I'm surprised."

"Why?" Kai huffed. "I think he was in an impossible situation." Did Marco think he was that much of a bastard?

Marco stepped back and sent Kai such a look of utter defeat it hurt. "So, you can forgive Charles for being in a situation not of his own making, but you can't forgive me for the same?" He didn't wait for an answer even if Kai could have thought of one. Kai opened his mouth to apologize but Marco just strode off.

Kai wanted to hit something. They were supposed to be drawing closer together, working things out, but if anything, things seemed to be getting worse.

Chapter Fourteen

Kai's stomach was still a little upset the next day, but he wasn't sick. He could quite easily put down the occasional bouts of nausea he'd had to the upset with Charles. He didn't need to worry about hiding it from Marco though because he'd barely seen him. Not that he would begrudge any time Marco spent with Charles. But he didn't think Marco even came into his room last night at all and he didn't know what to say to him, even if they could get a moment to talk. He sat with Emmett and Darriel that morning and even braved the bouncy chair for Maddox. It felt a little strange without his warm weight next to him.

"Kai?" He turned around to see Fox. It was three in the afternoon and they had just finished cleaning out some of the rooms. Isabelle—Nema's wife—had taken over the housekeeping side of things since the older couple who used to do it was travelling to see their grandchildren. "Is Marco here? Charles is upset and I don't know what to do." Neither probably did Kai, but they were a medic down because of him, so he could go see. He knew no one had seen Marco since that morning, and he was trying not to worry.

"What happened?" Kai asked. Fox toed the ground looking extremely uncomfortable. "What is it?" Kai prompted gently. He knew Fox had been really affected by the state Charles was in.

He huffed a breath out. "You know how Zeke reads to Darriel. Or used to," he added.

"Yes, of course," Kai replied as they walked.

Fox shrugged. "I dunno. I thought Charles might like the same, so I suggested it and he started crying. *Shit*," he snapped and abruptly turned and stormed off in the opposite direction. Kai cocked his head and thought hard as Fox disappeared. Fox thought Charles was angry with him, but Kai thought it was something else entirely. He didn't think Charles was used to kindness in any form. He cradled the sling Maddox was in, thankful he'd just been fed even if he wasn't asleep, and headed to Charles's room. He knocked, then let himself in. Charles was on his own because Fox had just left and Kai approached the bed, getting Maddox out of the sling as he did so.

"I think he's getting too heavy. My back's killing me." It wasn't, but he needed something to say.

Charles bent his head, but there was barely any reaction as he looked at Maddox, and Maddox could usually pull a smile from Charles, even a weak one.

"Fox thinks he upset you." Kai didn't prevaricate. There was no point. Charles didn't reply, simply turned away. "He offered to read to you because it was something Zeke, Emmett's dad, did for Darriel, one of the other omegas. Darriel's been on bed rest because he's at a risk of miscarriage and he's so bored. Fox was just offering the same."

Charles didn't reply, but Kai knew he was listening. Kai laid Maddox down next to the man. Charles was half-sitting with a bunch of pillows behind him. He'd slid down though and looked uncomfortable. "If you hold Maddox for me, I can try and sort those pillows for you." Not giving Charles a chance to refuse, Kai moved Maddox onto Charles's lap. Charles automatically clutched him when Kai let go, so he was steady. Kai fussed with the pillows but didn't take Maddox back. He didn't sit on the bed this time either like he usually did, just grabbed the chair.

Charles looked surprised, but then Maddox let out a funny kind of squawk for attention. Charles looked down at him immediately offering him his finger to hold. Maddox clutched it tight and tried to suck it. It was so unexpected Charles laughed hoarsely as if his throat was unaccustomed to such expressions of enjoyment. But then Kai supposed it wasn't. He took a deep breath and hoped he really wasn't going to screw this up, but no one seemed to be getting through to Charles. He might manage one protein shake and a few sips of water for the day if they were lucky, but he was wasting away before their eyes.

Emmett had told him it was only the strength of his shifter body that was keeping him alive, but as he couldn't actually shift and heal, this couldn't go on forever and they were rapidly running out of options.

"When Ryker asked me if I was okay with you coming here, I said no."

Charles froze. He didn't alter his grip on Maddox, but after a moment he raised distressed eyes to Kai.

"I remember you holding my head while they poured that crap down my throat and I couldn't get past that. But then I also remember you giving me privacy in the bathroom and telling Samson to stop because he was giving me too much. I saw your bruises, and Marco told me you risked a great deal to tell him how to undo the effects of the stuff." Kai fiddled with the blanket. "I made a ton of mistakes and you were a convenient target and I'm sorry." He met Charles's astonished gaze. "We omegas need to stick together. We—Emmett, Darriel and I—would very much like to spend more time together and to have you with us." He nodded to Maddox. "You have Maddox's seal of approval."

Charles swallowed with difficulty and looked down at Maddox. "How do you know them here?"

Kai wanted to dance. It was the most he had heard Charles say, but he was very careful not to react. He told Charles his story. Maddox snuggled quite happily against Charles and Kai helped prop Charles's arm on pillows so he wouldn't get too tired holding Maddox. Maddox yawned and Charles smiled. He gently grazed a finger down Maddox's cheek.

"And I've gone and screwed it up again."

"By living here?" Charles clarified.

"No. Ryker has permission from the council to name all omegas as pack so they can stay." That got another surprised look from Charles. "With Marco I mean. I very ably demonstrated I don't trust him again after he was willing to die for me." And then that story came out as well. They were interrupted by Chrissy who left a fresh protein shake, water and some of Dinah's muffins. Kai cut up a muffin into small pieces and left them on a plate. He didn't make a thing of it, but he made sure Charles could reach. Charles never tried for the muffins, but he was so distracted by listening to Kai's saga he finished his shake.

Maddox was asleep by this time, obviously bored of all the talking.

"Can I ask why Fox upset you?"

Charles kept his gaze on the baby. "What's his real name?"

"Fox?" Kai clarified. Charles nodded. "I honestly have no idea," Kai said. "I don't think I've heard anyone call him anything else." He tried to dredge up what else he knew. "He lives here alone and is part of the rescue squad."

"Rescue squad?"

Which of course was a whole other conversation, so Kai just supplied the brief details. He was more interested in what Fox had said to upset Charles.

Charles was silent for a while, obviously thinking. "It wasn't his fault. Nothing he said. He's been very kind." Kai was puzzled. There was something—Kai was sure—significant here that Charles wasn't saying. Since he'd so far managed success by being blunt, he tried again.

"Marco is convinced you want to go back and live with Samson even though I wish he was dead. I don't understand why he isn't to be honest. Regina is a badass." He huffed. "Anyway, I think he's wrong because no one would want to live with such a monster."

Charles met his eyes, sadness and defeat etched so deep in his psyche he looked like sorrow bled from him. "I have no choice. I have to return."

"Why?" Kai whispered, heart hammering and not a hundred percent sure he really wanted to know.

Charles swallowed. "Because it's the only chance I may have to get my babies back."

"Babies," Kai repeated. He didn't know why he was so astounded though, Charles was an omega.

Charles looked to the window. It was a nice room with a view of the trees and the lawn. After school there would be some pups playing right there.

"I had eleven, *have* eleven. And each one was taken from me a few days after their birth. Sold. Samson promised me the next one I could keep, but he stopped touching me and I'm too damaged now, I guess. I thought if I stayed I might find out where they went." He shook his head. "Or I knew if I left, I absolutely would never find out where they are."

Kai pressed his lips together, eyes smarting. *Eleven.* He couldn't even begin to imagine how heartbreaking that was. Losing Maddox had nearly killed him, but *eleven?*

"And that's why I got upset with Fox. It was a sweet offer, but it's something I've dreamed about. To have the chance of reading a story to my own child." Tears rolled down Charles's face and Kai climbed up in bed beside him, Maddox asleep between them. He put an arm around Charles's thin shoulders and Charles turned his face into him. They both wept for a long time.

Chapter Fifteen

Three days later Marco was out of ideas. He'd studiously made sure he saw to Charles until late every night and made sure he was gone before Kai woke up in the morning. Their only interaction was the shift-change as Emmett called it when Kai, always with Maddox, took a turn with Charles. Charles was a little better—or he was when Kai was there. He didn't speak to anyone else and Kai was trying to spend as much time with him as possible. He was eating—if you could call protein shakes food, but he refused everything else. Most nights Marco didn't sleep at all. The first night when he'd woken just before dawn to Kai wrapped around him like plastic wrap, he'd known for his own sanity he couldn't do it anymore. So, he dozed on the couch or when he was desperate took himself to bed in the other room.

But then he didn't sleep because Kai and Maddox were too far away and he couldn't rest without Kai safe in his arms.

He was writing his notes up in the clinic that morning when he felt someone behind him. He turned to see Ryker looking at him with defeat and apology written all over him.

"What is it?" His heart thudded in his chest.

"They've let them go."

All Marco heard for a moment was white noise. Eventually he gasped, "Why?" Because he knew exactly who Ryker was talking about.

"Harker successfully argued that Kai didn't belong to a pack, so no pack could exact a retribution challenge, and he was fairly bought and paid for. They let Samson go because they deemed the debt paid in losing the omega."

Marco frowned. "But Kai's—"

"Not at the time he wasn't," Ryker interrupted. "I got the pack ratified after Kai left." Marco hung his head. Something else that had been his fault.

"But we have a bigger problem," he said softly.

Marco met his eyes. But he knew. He *fucking* new.

"The council contacted your mother to see if the clan would challenge on your behalf." Ryker paused.

"And?" Marco prodded almost fatalistically.

"She said no."

Marco let familiar anger race through him. "Regina doesn't trust her." Because that was the understatement of the century. "And I can't leave now because of Trina." Even if he thought it would make Kai safer.

"So, you'd leave me, but you wouldn't leave now because of your *sister*?"

Marco and Ryker both swung around at the furious voice to see Kai's ashen face.

"No," Marco said. "I didn't mean it like that." Knowing that was exactly how it sounded. Ryker shot a sympathetic smile at Marco and left the clinic, closing the door behind him.

"What did you mean then?" Kai whispered, the hurt shimmering in his eyes and threatening to brim over.

"Every time I open my mouth I say something wrong, but what I meant to say was even if I thought it would make you safer to leave—because that's the only reason I would choose to go—I have to be here for Trina for the same thing."

Kai took a breath. "I came to talk to you because we're getting nowhere. You keep asking me to trust you, but then you prove that I can't."

"You can't?" Marco repeated than noticed Kai didn't have his usual sling on. "Where's Maddox?" Marco asked in alarm.

"With Dinah and Emmett in the kitchen and it's killing me, so listen up."

"I would do anything for you."

"Except give me what I really want," Kai said gently putting a hand to Marco's cheek.

Marco frowned. "What—"

"I want a guarantee you will stay. That you're going to make a family with me. That you're not going to run because you think in some mad screwy way that will save me. It won't. And I keep expecting to turn around and find you gone."

"And what about your guarantees?" Marco shot back, and all the agony of the past few weeks, the past few years came pouring out. "I offered you the bond and you threw it back in my face. You denied *me*. You're happy for me to dance in attendance. To care for your son like he was my own. To keep you safe every fucking night until you decide if I'm good enough or not." Marco stepped right up to Kai. "I was willing to fucking *die* for you. Don't you think you've punished me enough?"

Marco slammed his notes on the table, pushed past Kai and started running. He held off his cat long enough to text Chrissy and stash his phone and clothes. Then he gave in and for once exulted as the power rushed through him. He wasn't interested in coming back.

He intended on going far enough this time that not even Ryker would come for him, but then he paused. Wasn't this *exactly* what Kai had just accused him of? Half of him wanted to turn around and go sort this out with Kai once and for all, but there was something else he needed to do as well. He couldn't spend the rest of his life looking over his shoulder.

It took him barely forty minutes—as fast as his cat could go—before he let himself into one of the stocked rescue cabins dotted all over the area for shifters. He helped himself to water and some clothes, then made a decision he hoped he wasn't going to regret and accessed his accounts with one of the burner phones available.

He wanted to text Kai, but this needed a different sort of communication. Six hours and a plane ride later, he walked up to the luxury apartments in front of him and let himself into a fancy reception area. He knew the security guards manning the foyer were clan. Nicholas might not be female, but he was still of the Panthera's line and would be protected. He didn't recognize either guard though, so he simply walked to the desk.

"Please inform Nicholas Stanza he has a guest."

Both their eyes narrowed. "Is he expecting you...?"

"Marco Stanza." Marco got a certain amount of satisfaction when the older of the two clearly recognized his name. The second guard stepped away to make the call and within a minute he gestured to the elevators. Marco followed him and noted he inserted a key then pressed a button that wasn't numbered. He nodded politely and stepped out. The elevator was as fast as Marco had expected. He stepped out into an entryway with a single door ahead of him. He'd barely taken a step when it was flung open and Nicholas was there. For a moment they just drunk each other in, and then in a totally uncharacteristic move, Nicholas opened his arms wide and Marco stepped into them. He breathed Nicholas in for a moment and embraced his brother, then Nicholas stepped back, suspicious tears in his eyes.

"I can't believe you're here. Come in." He waved Marco inside. Marco took in the luxury in one glance. From the full wall window showing most of the city to the paintings on the other three walls—each one he was sure cost hundreds of thousands of dollars—to the jeans and silk shirt Nicholas wore that were no doubt Balenciaga or something similar.

"I can't believe you're here," he said again. "Can I get you something? Coffee? Water? Beer?"

Marco shook his head, not knowing where to start. He had to find out what was going on without giving Nicholas any information at all. "I'm in a pack." He knew that wasn't telling him anything the Panthera didn't already know.

"A pack?" Nicholas repeated. "You mean a clan?" He understood Nicholas's confusion. Panthers didn't change clans like wolves changed packs. They stayed in the clan they were born in or they left. Those were the only two choices.

"I mean a pack. Mixed shifters." He sat down and tried to at least look relaxed. "I'm a trained medic and work for the ranger service up in the Blue Ridge Mountain area of North Carolina. I've joined the pack permanently as their medic and"—he sighed deliberately—"I'm sick of running Nicholas. I want to put down roots. I just want to be sure she's not going to come after me." There, that sounded reasonable.

Nicholas blinked almost stupidly. "Settle down," he repeated.

He shrugged. "I've been running since you helped me escape. I'm done."

Nicholas blew out a breath and raked a hand over his face. "Honestly? I don't think she'd care. If she wanted you dead, it would have happened. She has other things on her mind." Marco waited, but he didn't elaborate. He guessed he had the same trust issues with him, if he even knew Trina was missing. And Marco had been gone a long time. If he was Nicholas, he might be suspicious.

"How's Dad?"

Nate's shoulders slumped. "Same. Books and crosswords. You know how he is."

"And Nate?"

His look became more guarded, bitter almost. "He's fine. Wishes he was born a girl, but—" Nicholas shrugged. Marco frowned. Nate had always been more like Dad. Nose in a book. Anything to avoid a confrontation. The thought he could have any sort of ambition was quite frankly ludicrous.

"Since when?"

Nicholas sighed. "He's changed, Marco. He follows her everywhere and she started including him in things. I mean *planning*. She'd even started asking his advice. He lives up at the house."

That did surprise Marco. "But wasn't he given a house?" Like they all were. Nicholas snorted.

"Yeah, somewhere, but he doesn't live in it. Prefers to hang out with mommy dearest." He shrugged. "She just uses me as muscle."

"Enforcer?" But he knew. Nicholas had replaced him.

"In full cat. She thinks it makes her look good." Which is what she had done to him. Nicholas still hadn't mentioned Trina, but he didn't know Marco now, not really. And he had even less reason to trust him knowing how much Marco despised the family. It also sounded like he wasn't in their mother's confidence, unlike Nate.

"Can you stay?"

Marco shook his head. "Sorry. I've got two omegas about to deliver and one will be tricky." It was a good excuse.

Nicholas blinked again. "What, you're like a midwife?"

He grinned. "We have a full clinic, and I love it."

"That makes sense. You always did like taking care of people." Marco stood. He wanted to get back to Kai. They had to talk. He shouldn't have lost his temper.

Marco hesitated. "I'm sorry you're having to put up with all of this on your own, but surely she can't have that many years left?" He frowned. "I mean I've been away a long time." He was fishing, but Nicholas simply shook his head.

"Still too many." Nicholas smiled sheepishly. "I'm not as strong as you."

And Marco didn't dare push anymore. "Give me your number," Nicholas said and they swapped contact information even though it wasn't his phone. He could make an excuse though. "Are you sure I can't persuade you to stay? At least stay for dinner?"

Marco hugged his brother again and said goodbye, sure someone would be on Trina's side when she needed it. He didn't like the sound of what Nate had become though. He rode down the elevator again and stepped out into the foyer. The same two guards nodded politely as he left. He held his hand out for a cab only to turn as he heard his name shouted behind him. It was Nicholas.

"Let me drive you. I have something you need to know."

Marco was surprised and wondered if he was going to tell him about Trina, but he waited patiently while a driver emerged from the lower ground parking lot and handed Nicholas the keys. He slid inside, unsurprised by the expensive Porsche. "What is it?"

Nicholas swallowed. "We have a sister."

"What?" Marco asked with the right amount of surprise. "How old is she?"

"Thirteen," Nicholas bit out, "and she's missing."

"Missing," Marco repeated inanely. "How? When—"

"Mother says she's packed her off to a northern clan for safety." He chewed his thumb as he joined traffic heading for the airport. "But she won't tell me which one."

Marco frowned. "And you don't have any contacts?"

"Not that I trust not to tell her, no."

Marco blew out a breath and pretended to be considering things. "Why don't you think Mother is telling you the truth?"

"There was an attack at the house."

He glanced at Nicholas. This sounded more like Trina's story. "An attack?"

He jerked a nod. "I was dealing with the typical banned mate bullshit —" He sent Marco a horrified look. "Shit, I'm sorry."

"It's okay. Go on."

"Well, when we got there everyone had gone and there was supposed to be this fight going on. I didn't like it, so I called Trina and told her to get into the crawl space we devised under the kitchen."

Marco debated asking Nicholas why he thought his thirteen-year-old sister would need a hiding place, but decided his brother wasn't so stupid.

"When I got back there were enforcers all over the place. Mother was injured and so was Slate." Slate had been their housekeeper. Marco didn't know the guy still worked for them. "Anyway, they both shifted and were okay, but we think it was an attack by the Columbus Clan. They've butted heads with Mother for years and with Trina missing she wouldn't have an heir. The closest is like three years."

"When I got there, Mother said she'd sent Katrina away to safety. At least until she's fourteen."

Marco didn't point out that their mother had a hundred enforcers she could immediately call on if she needed to. He knew Nicholas thought moving Trina was ridiculous. That was why he was suspicious in the first place.

"What does Dad say?" He missed the old man. Nicholas scoffed.

"He's too busy doing crosswords to care." Marco didn't respond, but in a lot of ways it was true. He'd never decided if Dad was woefully ignorant or deliberately obtuse.

"What are you going to do?"

Nicholas pulled into the terminal drop off area. He pulled up, put the car in park and turned to Marco. "There's nothing I can do. You know that."

Marco studied him. "I'd love to help, but I literally know no one who would even talk to me from any clan."

Nicholas sighed theatrically. "Couldn't you make something up?"

Marco wanted to laugh because it was ridiculous. There was no clan that would risk a Panthera's ire by talking to a son who had turned his back on her, but he had a flight to catch and arguing wouldn't get him anywhere. "Let me make some inquiries. I'll let you know."

Marco was thoughtful as he entered the terminal. He didn't know what to think and decided to ask Regina at the earliest opportunity. He made the same detour back to the pack house. He left the fake shifter ID he had used at the cabin—because panthers couldn't carry wallets without help—and resolved to replace the small amount of cash he had taken the next day. He shifted after memorizing Nicholas's cell number and ran back to where his phone and clothes were and dressed quickly. Three missed calls from Ryker and a reply to the text he'd sent to Chrissy saying he would be back tonight but late. He called Ryker before he pocketed the phone. "I'll be back in around thirty minutes."

"Good. Everything's okay," Ryker confirmed. Marco breathed out a sigh of relief. He jogged all the way back to the pack house.

It was Chrissy—unsurprisingly—who met him on the steps. "I talked to Ryker." He wanted to ask where Kai was.

"They've got Red moving furniture. Started just after you called a few minutes ago."

Marco felt the blood drain from his face. Kai was moving rooms? Was it to be separate from him now that he knew he was coming back? Chrissy patted him on his arm. "Don't be a flake. Go man up and help." But what if his help was the last thing Kai wanted? With leaden feet he walked towards the omega wing where they had slept the last three weeks. The door to his room was open and Red and Fox staggered out with his bed. Marco did a double take. He should have known Kai wasn't going anywhere. Obviously he would want to stay with the rest of the omegas. *He* was moving. His chest already ached with the loss of Kai.

"What can I do?" Marco asked.

"Thank fuck!" Red exclaimed. "You can rescue me from omegas who decide they want to move to the opposite end of the damn house when all normal people would be going to bed already."

Marco blinked and looked down at his bed. "But that's mine."

"Duh," Red replied. "And apparently it's a better mattress. You planning on sleeping somewhere your mate isn't?" He scoffed as if that was the most ridiculous thing he'd ever heard.

Marco didn't get the chance to ask Red what the hell he meant, because he instinctively looked up at a small sound from the doorway. Kai, still clutching Maddox, stood at the entrance to the second room, staring right at him. Distress was so apparent in his green-brown eyes that Marco just wanted to hug him close and tell him everything was going to be okay. But he couldn't. He didn't have the right to do that.

"We're leaving this bed here, right?" Emmett's voice carried from inside. Kai didn't reply and another couple of seconds Emmett appeared. "Do you—*oh*," he said spotting Marco and grinning. "Perfect timing. We need the changing table and the rocking chair moved." Marco reluctantly wrenched his eyes away from Kai to Emmett. He stared at him as if Emmett was speaking in a foreign language and Emmett grinned and looked over at Red. "Give me the pillows and I'll follow you."

Red sniggered. "But alpha-mate, don't you think those pillows are too heavy for you to carry?"

Emmett narrowed his eyes. "Do you want me to sit on that bed while you move it?"

"Maybe just show us where you want it?" Red grumbled and they all walked off.

Marco turned to stare at Kai. Kai cleared his throat. "There's a family suite on the other side of the kitchen. It's where Emmett and Ryker stayed before they moved to their cabin. It's bigger and closer to the clinic."

Marco still couldn't find the words he needed. "For me?" he said slowly.

"For both of us." Kai bit his lip. "I'm so sorry. I regretted it as soon as you'd left. I'm messing everything up." Marco—very gently because of Maddox—drew Kai close, tilted his chin up with the tip of one finger and kissed him on the mouth. He tried to put every feeling, every hope, every expectation he had into that meeting of lips against lips, and Kai returned it. When Maddox cho-choo'd he drew back smiling. Kai was giving him another chance. He wanted to punch the air.

Kai gazed at him. "I was afraid you weren't coming back. That you would decide I was too much trouble. And you were right," Kai said softly. "It's like I've been holding you to an impossible standard," he added. Marco dropped a kiss on Maddox's head. Sheer gratitude making him speechless.

"We have lots of things to talk about, but how about you let me help the guys, then we can get settled in?"

Kai looked scared to death and that hit him harder than anything Ryker had told him.

"I just want you to know one thing. One very important thing."

Kai raised worried eyes to him, and Marco smoothed the little lines on his forehead away with his thumbs. "There's no rush." He rubbed a thumb down Kai's jaw. "Hell, the way I feel I'm not planning on letting you out of my sight for a long time." It was obviously the right thing to say because Kai grinned.

"Let's help move everything so we can have some time to ourselves."

Yes. That was the one thing they definitely needed. Marco just wasn't sure with the threats of the clan, Harker, and Samson hanging over them they were actually going to get it.

Chapter Sixteen

Kai was filthy and tired. And of course Maddox decided he was wide awake *thank you very much* and wanted entertaining when all Kai wanted was some quiet and very alone time with Marco. Marco chuckled softly and plucked Maddox from Kai's arms and nodded to the shower. "Take your time," he ordered.

Kai only had a tiny spark of anxiety, which he quickly squashed because he'd seen Marco very deliberately lock both the main door and the patio door to their rooms so he knew no one was getting in. And for the first time, Kai wished Maddox was asleep for another reason. Because he wanted Marco to join him in the shower.

He'd quite like Marco to touch him anywhere he wished. His skin was starved. His heart was starved. What had he been thinking? He'd done nothing but push Marco away when he was the best thing that had ever happened to him. He turned on the water and wondered if Marco had eaten. If he should offer to get him something? Maybe coffee?

Overwhelming nausea suddenly washed over him. Kai threw out a hand in complete panic to anchor himself and breathed rapidly through his mouth to banish it. He'd swear, but that would involve moving his lips and they were very firmly closed. He could say fuck very loudly in his head though.

His idea for coffee had very quickly brought up the scent in his imagination, and the taste as it ran down his throat. *Fuck, fuck, fuck.* That was almost as bad as the hot chocolate. Kai could feel the blood drain from his face and his dinner come up to meet it. He barely made it to the toilet and just thanked anyone that was listening the sound of the water drowned out the sound of him being sick.

He collapsed almost onto the floor and leaned his head back against the wall. His head was swimming and his belly was still roiling. He shut his eyes for a moment and the next thing he knew strong arms were lifting him up off the floor. "Kai? What's wrong?" Worry threaded its way very audibly through Marco's words and Kai tried and failed to hold back a sob.

"Sweetheart?" Marco sat down on the floor clutching Kai to him. Kai buried his head in Marco's shirt, conscious of the fact that he hadn't brushed his teeth and just wanted to die.

"Maddox has been asleep for ages and I was going to join you, but then I thought I'd better check because you seemed to be taking a long time and it isn't like you." He stood and turned the shower off. Kai huffed. He had that right. He'd been so panicked with the thought of Chrissy being alone with Maddox that day he'd barely paused to grab a towel.

"How do you feel?"

Kai took an easier breath. "A bit better. It's just been a long couple of days I guess." Marco didn't reply and Kai didn't dare look him in the face. "I need a shower and to brush my teeth."

Marco kissed the top of his head. "Do you feel like you can stand?"

"Yes," Kai croaked out. Marco stood, then simply picked him up with seemingly no effort, walked into the bedroom, deposited him on the bed and shot him a stern look.

"Stay there."

Kai watched as Marco disappeared into the bathroom and turned on the water again. He came back at the same time as he was pulling his shirt over his head. If Kai hadn't felt so gross he could have appreciated Marco's powerful muscles and the sleek cat-like sway of his hips. Kai blinked as Marco shoved down his pants and Kai really *really* wished he felt better.

Marco smiled gently, almost as if Kai had said that aloud, then he scooped Kai up and carried him to the bathroom settling him down gently in front of the sink. Kai brushed his teeth and immediately felt fresher.

Then Marco simply stripped Kai and Kai didn't have either the energy or the inclination to object. Marco eased him into the shower and when Kai reached for the body wash, Marco hushed him and told him to stay still. Kai closed his eyes at the first touch of Marco's hands on his skin. Marco started at his feet and moved up his legs. He quickly gave Kai's now awake cock some loving attention. When his hands moved higher, Kai groaned pathetically. Marco didn't leave a single inch of Kai's skin untouched. He even washed his hair. Kai was floating when he'd finished, turned on *yes* because this was Marco, but more lulled into a blissful state of comfort by such tender care. Marco made him feel...he didn't know, *important* maybe? Like he might actually be worth something to somebody.

"Thank you." Kai's voice broke. No one had ever done that, taken such good care of him. All his life he had felt like he should apologize for who and what he was, but Marco made him feel *precious*. He dried him just as carefully and settled him in bed before getting in and pulling him close.

"You aren't ever allowed to change your mind now," Kai whispered when he was convinced Marco had drifted off to sleep. "You can't let go."

"Never," Marco rumbled back and tightened the arm he'd laid possessively across Kai's hips. Then he raised his head a little to kiss the side of Kai's cheek and swiped him with his tongue.

"Eww," Kai chuckled sleepily.

"Just so you know," Marco said. "I've licked you so you're mine."

Kai could hear the satisfaction in his voice. He was still laughing when he went to sleep.

Kai woke at Maddox's cry. It was still dark outside, but the warmth of Marco's body spooning his made his heart melt. He shuffled and Marco moved. "I'll get him, you go pee or whatever." Kai didn't need to be told twice, he went, plus got in another sneaky tooth brushing because he felt okay this morning. Marco was just snapping closed Maddox's onesie when he returned, and he climbed back into bed and held his arms out. The bottle warmer dinged after a moment and Marco handed it over, then he went into the bathroom. Kai kissed his son and told him how beautiful he was, and whispered he'd be absolutely perfect if he would give Daddy at least another hour before he needed him again. Not that Kai was planning on getting any more sleep.

The baby gods must have been smiling on him because by the time Marco came out of the bathroom and made up another bottle for the next round, Maddox had emptied the current one and was doing a rather good impression of a guppy. His eyes were very firmly shut though.

Marco grinned and picked him up, kissing his forehead softly and settled him back in his crib.

Kai scooted over and made a big show of fluffing pillows *because what if he isn't interested?* He could be tired. He probably was tired. Crap, he was probably exhausted.

"Kai?"

Kai suddenly focused on Marco who had managed to climb into bed while he was off in his own world worrying. Marco lay on his back and stretched out his arm. Kai didn't need to be asked twice and he snuggled in, loving how Marco's arm came around his back possessively. They were so close now. Marco's warm breaths puffed into his hair as Kai laid his head on Marco's chest. Kai could hear Marco's heartbeat. A big steady thump-thump in his ear that seemed to hold him as safe as the arms around him. He moved. It could be taken as a casual resettling to get himself comfortable or an absentminded shuffling like everyone did just after they got into bed. To get their position just right...he blew out a steady breath feeling his cock pressed against Marco's hip. Marco's own steady breathing hitched a little. Kai wasn't brave enough to search out Marco's cock with his fingers to see if their proximity was having the same effect on him as it was on Kai's body. He wanted it to though. He felt the kiss that Marco pressed onto his hair and looked up. Their lips were maybe three inches apart and Kai narrowed his gaze on them knowing Marco's shifter sight, even in the dim room, would see what he was doing. He waited a beat and nothing happened. Marco didn't move, didn't speak.

So he licked his lips encouragingly. That didn't seem to work either.

Taking every scrap of courage he had, he inched higher. Marco didn't move. They were almost touching and everything in Kai seemed to teeter on a knife's edge until Marco dipped his head a fraction and their mouths met. He'd kissed Marco before. Once in a drugged haze and plenty of times after they had gotten home. But this almost felt like the first time, the soft touch of warm lips meeting his was like coming home. He lifted up and leaned over Marco, not taking his lips away for one moment.

Marco's hands—now free—slid through his hair and anchored Kai's head still as if he was going to pull away. If Kai's mouth hadn't been so distracted, he'd have laughed at the absurdity. He moaned softly, encouragingly, and rocked until he could feel Marco's hard length and exulted knowing it was because of him. He broke away and sucked along Marco's jawline as Marco obediently lifted it for him. Marco's hands smoothed their way down his back and under the waistband of his sleep pants. "Too many clothes," he whispered. Marco hummed in seeming agreement as he worked them down. Kai's heart was tripping and racing as Marco's hands slid over his ass and scraped his thighs as he took them off. "Now yours," he said against the warm skin of Marco's throat.

Marco rolled, fast, very fast, but he cushioned Kai's body as he turned him. Kai almost whimpered, luxuriating in the feeling of being trapped under all that strength. "Are you sure?"

Kai wriggled invitingly. His hole ached with the thought of Marco filling him. "Yes."

"I don't just mean for that," Marco said and met Kai's gaze. "This isn't casual. I want all in. I want us to be mates and to make a family. I want Maddox to be my son. I want everything with you."

Kai's heart swelled so much he thought it might burst. This gorgeous man wanted him for keeps, and Kai wanted him right back. "I won't be easy. I still have a lot of problems with trust."

Marco smiled gently and rewarded the statement with a kiss. "I know, sweetheart. And I love that you can tell me. I've spent all my life running from the situation I was born into, but I'm done. It might need to be faced and I hate that I'm putting you in possible danger, but I tried letting you go and look how that turned out."

They both chuckled. Lips against lips as they laughed together. "I'm stronger than I look," Kai said because he didn't want inequality. He didn't want Marco to ever feel like he had to hide things.

"You're the strongest person I know," Marco whispered. "You amaze me." Marco skimmed his lips over Kai's mouth, his throat, and worked his way down his chest, carefully trapping one nipple in his mouth and rimming it with his tongue.

"Uh," Kai made a startled noise as lust suddenly shot from his nipple to his cock. "Fuck," he whispered weakly and Marco raised his head.

"Like?" Kai nodded in bemusement, then closed his eyes and arched in a desperate plea for more. He was stunned because his nipples had never been his thing. He knew some people got off on them but—he whined at the first touch of Marco's teeth, squirming for more. He didn't know what to do with his hands, so he held the back of Marco's head and scraped his nails through Marco's hair. He heard the rumbled approval from Marco's throat. His cock was rigid and nearing uncomfortable and he wriggled for relief, gasping at the gorgeous friction.

Marco reached lower and the first touch of his fingers nearly had Kai shooting. "Please," he begged. "Please." His hole clenched; his body throbbed. Marco lifted up, meeting his gaze and their eyes locked. Kai loved him. He wanted him with a passion bordering on desperation, but it was different this time because his heart was finally on board. Marco bent Kai's legs and lowered his head. Kai moaned as Marco mouthed his belly and groin, and he did his best to thrust his hips invitingly. Marco chuckled and clamped a large hand over Kai's thigh to anchor him. Kai moaned as Marco's finger finally breached his hole. "Fuck," Kai offered weakly, his mind, his body spiraling out of control. He could feel his slick, feel Marco swipe his finger around the rim. Kai panted, his heart racing towards a finish line that was maddeningly still out of sight. Frustration made him whimper once more, but then Marco pushed a finger inside and it seemed like all of Kai's body clamped down. "More," he demanded, and soon two weren't enough either.

Marco knelt up, one hand on Kai's inner thigh to steady him, the other on his own cock to position it. Marco briefly closed his eyes and Kai gazed in wonder at the complete satisfaction on his face, then Marco moved and all thoughts fled entirely from Kai's brain to be replaced by pure need. Marco pushed slowly, the relentless burn and pressure registering but almost at a distance because there seemed to be nothing else in Kai's universe but his love for this man and the urgent need for Marco to take him, make him his. He could even feel the seductive throb of blood under the skin of his neck as he craved the bite that would follow. Marco pushed until he was fully seated, then breathed for a moment, before taking, *demanding* a kiss that ravaged Kai's mouth. Kai was incapable of speech, even begging as Marco pulled back then pushed in quickly. He paused, then did it again and again until Kai found his voice and pleases and yesses and sounds he didn't recognize spilled from his throat as Marco relentlessly pushed him to the edge.

Then, just as he was ready to jump off, Marco found that special place on his neck and bit hard. White light blinded Kai and he could do nothing but feel. He came so hard he felt it down to his toes and felt the pulsing inside him as Marco did the same. As a teen, he'd heard the whispered stories that when you met your true mate the bond that joined you was a living, breathing thing. Something that tethered you to another soul where both hearts beat as one and only for each other.

His last conscious thought was that it had been true.

Kai opened his eyes sometime later and smiled. Marco was sitting up, leaning against the pillows and Maddox was lying with his back resting against Marco's raised and bent legs. He looked for all the world like he was talking back to Marco with his oo-oohs and his little shrieks and all the fist waving. Kai raised his head and Marco, noticing, bent and captured his lips in a steamy kiss.

Kai's hands flew to his neck when his mark pulsed as Marco kissed him.

Marco drew back and gazed at him. "It looks good on you." Kai shivered when Marco grazed his finger over it and his cock jerked a little. Marco's pupils deepened as he took in the reaction Kai couldn't hide. "Later," he promised. "Let's get up, bathe this little monster, and go get some breakfast."

Kai's belly did a little lurch and he immediately told it to behave.

Marco met his gaze. "And then we're going to the clinic because I want to check you over."

The morning didn't go quite as planned though as Marco had to deal with one of the pup's suddenly shifting for the first time in the middle of his lessons and tipping the desk over onto another one. It had been chaos for a few minutes until Nema dealt with the rest of the pups so Marco could see to the injured one. Ryker had been summoned to see to his new wolf and he had taken him out on his first run. Darriel, Emmett and Kai were sitting in the kitchen in their usual comfy corner. Kai was trying to avoid the smell of coffee by sipping his orange juice and Calvin bounced in wanting to show Emmett the drawing he had done at school. They all admired it and Calvin bounced back out again armed with three lunch boxes for him and his two drawing buddies.

"How's the gamma squad shaping up?" Darriel asked wriggling to try and get his huge belly in a more comfortable position.

Kai chuckled and lifted up Maddox. "You gonna be a gamma, sweetie, or maybe an alpha? Grr," Kai teased and Emmett looked up from his phone.

"Dad's landed. He's going to come straight here." He glanced at Darriel who shrugged.

"I haven't time to worry about stubborn men," he said and patted his belly. "I'm too concerned about stubborn babies." Which was true. After being at risk of losing his twins for so many weeks, he was now officially overdue and they all knew Marco was concerned. He had no experience with overdue shifter babies as it was unheard of, and he'd told Darriel if he didn't go into labor soon Dinah was going to have to interfere.

That pronouncement had met with blank looks. Dinah who was also with them at the time started chuckling and mentioning disgusting stuff like castor oil. All three of them wrinkled their noses in horror.

"Are you sure it's only twins?" Kai asked gazing at Darriel's huge belly. Darriel huffed and tried again to get comfortable.

"Ooh I got a new one," Emmett waved his hand excitedly. They both groaned. Emmett had been driving them crazy with pregnancy jokes. "What type of bird helps you deliver babies?"

Kai raised his eyebrows. "The stork?"

Emmett grinned. "*Correct!* But what bird stops you from getting pregnant in the first place?"

Kai glanced at Darriel who shrugged.

"The swallow!" Emmett let out a peal of laughter and Kai rolled his eyes. Darriel took a couple of seconds then started giggling which set them all off.

"And now I've got to pee," Darriel wailed which made them all laugh harder. Emmett stood and helped ease Darriel up off the chair. He took a step then froze and looked down at the baggy sleep pants he was wearing, which was the only thing he could get around his middle. "I'm wet," he said in a horrified voice. Kai and Emmett took one look at each other.

"Sit him back down," Kai directed. "I'll go get Marco."

Four hours later Kai sat holding Emmeline and Emmett was holding Karina. Both girls named after their dad's best friends Darriel told them before yawning and announcing he needed a nap. They were both fed and asleep, so Kai and Emmett put both babies in their cribs, picked up the car seats Ryker was guarding in the corner and tiptoed out. Marco kissed Kai softly and said he wouldn't be long. They both saw Zeke at the same time as he pushed himself off the wall.

"How is he?"

"Asleep," Emmett said. "Why don't you visit in a couple of hours?"

Zeke didn't reply immediately, but bent and kissed Josie's cheek, then

Emmett's. "I have to get back. I'll see you later." And he turned and walked out. Emmett sighed and looked at Kai.

"Stubborn alphas," they both said in unison. Laughing, they went to get something to eat.

Chapter Seventeen

Marco had waited patiently all month, but it seemed that even Chrissy was getting suspicious now. He knew full well that Emmett and Dinah had worked it out and probably Darriel.

He just had no idea when his obstinate *utterly gorgeous* omega was finally going to admit he was pregnant. Kai had happily sat while Marco had poked and prodded him the morning after Darriel had delivered, but Marco had chickened out of actually suggesting Kai take a pregnancy test because he wanted Kai to tell him himself.

His sickness had abated. He'd never suffered it in the morning which made since because Marco knew so called "morning" sickness, even for females, was a tiny percentage of the actual problem. There were a lot more incidences of sickness at different times of the day, but Marco had quickly worked out it was triggered by certain foods with Kai. And by the evening he definitely looked a little green to the point that Marco had taken over Maddox's evening feeding. Milk, anything creamy, and coffee, all seemed to set Kai off, so Marco had spent the month making sure his mate got all the nutrients he needed in more creative ways.

And no, not that. Marco sniggered to himself. Not at night anyway.

Thankfully Kai was always bright-eyed in the morning and *very* horny. Marco had never had so much sex in his entire life.

"What are you grinning at?"

Marco looked up from his laptop to see Zeke and smiled. "How's Trina?"

"Too damned intelligent," Zeke chuckled. "She's powering through eleventh grade math." Marco joined in Zeke's amusement. He wished he could see her, but he didn't dare risk it. "I've got some more security measures I'd like to go through with the team."

"I can't thank you enough."

Zeke waved it away as if it was nothing. "How are Darriel and the girls?" Marco hesitated but Zeke barreled on. "I know you can't tell me anything private. Just in general?" Marco felt like shit not being able to share a lot, especially with how much Zeke was doing for him, to say nothing for the organization as a whole, but he took patient privacy seriously.

"He's up and about. The twins are doing great."

Zeke's shoulders sagged in relief. "That's good to know."

There was an awkward pause and Marco wasn't sure how to fill it. "I'm surprised you didn't see him when you came in. I think they're all outside."

"I saw him," Zeke said almost in defeat and leaned against the counter. "They were just going inside, but Emmett hung back. I told him I would come and kiss my granddaughter in a few." He winced. "Fuck, that makes me sound too old."

Marco thought about that statement and what Kai had told him. That they thought—or Darriel did—that he had rejected him because Zeke was still in love with Emmett's mom, but Marco suddenly wondered if that was true. He'd probably seen more of their interactions together than anyone else when he had been treating Darriel, and while Zeke had been caring, he had never seemed paternal or brotherly. He could be wrong though. He'd made enough mistakes with Kai. And he happened to know Zeke was forty-four, so it hardly made him ready for his pension. Then he registered exactly what Zeke had said.

"Too old for what?"

Zeke focused on him. "Huh?"

"You said it made you sound *too* old."

Zeke flushed a little and shrugged. "Maybe I should amend that to being old enough to know better."

"We can all say that," Marco pointed out. He got his files together and debated breaking a confidence. Well, it wasn't exactly a confidence. Strictly speaking it was hearsay which might be worse. "Look, please feel free to tell me to fuck off and mind my own business, but according to what I've been told, you and Darriel aren't spending time together because he's a guy and you'll never get over losing Emmett's mom." He braced himself, almost expecting Zeke to take a swing at him, but his jaw dropped comically instead.

"What?"

Marco didn't bother repeating it, he knew by Zeke's bewildered expression he'd heard. "Maybe you need to have a conversation if he has that wrong."

Zeke stared at the floor. "I'm still more than twenty years older than him."

"You do know that the bond would increase your life expectancy?" Maybe he didn't.

Zeke raised his head and met Marco's gaze. "But it can't reverse things. It can't take away a twenty-three-year age gap."

"That's true," Marco conceded. "But I've personally found that assumptions are very dangerous things. It took me way too long to get my head out of my ass and I nearly lost Kai because of it."

Zeke nodded. "I said I'd come and get you. The others are waiting for us in the meeting room." Marco accepted the change of subject with alacrity and followed him out.

"So, what new security measures?" Ryker asked as soon as Marco, Chrissy, Red and Zeke had all sat down. Liam and TJ both wanted to carry on working for the rangers and the rescue squad really needed them there, so they would be alerted if there were any problems with shifters. Sam was away at an emergency medical training course which was a good thing, and Fox was...actually, where *was* Fox? But Marco knew. Somehow his mate had sorted out whatever had gone on between Fox and Charles, and Fox seemed to spend most off his off-duty hours with the man. He'd even seen them playing chess a few days ago. Charles barely ate enough to keep himself alive, but he was still with them thanks largely to Kai and Maddox, and now Fox. Charles didn't really talk to anyone else. It would be a slow process and they were all still expecting some sort of backlash from Harker and Samson. Although maybe they'd be lucky.

"An exit strategy. I've had an escape hatch built." Marco dragged his thoughts back to what they were talking about and gaped, not a hundred percent certain what Zeke had just said.

"But you live in the penthouse," Chrissy pointed out. "How long is this escape hatch?"

Zeke grinned. "I bought one of the apartments two floors down with a fake name through the company that Seth's sister works for. It's going to be used for their employees when they have meetings with clients in the area. It's being designed with a separate entrance hidden behind a dummy electrical panel. It will be completed next week."

"That's amazing," Chrissy responded. Marco was still speechless. Zeke shrugged. "We thought about a safe room, but decided that since most shifters don't like tight spaces for extended periods this was the way to go."

Which was true. Many shifters would balk at being shut up. Their animals would rebel. "So, would Trina know how to use it?" Marco asked.

"She will be shown. We can't share this with many because it only takes one person to talk for it to be useless, but I thought the investment was worth it for another few months. It was simply a case of rerouting some air conditioning ducting." He looked at Ryker. "You, for example, wouldn't fit." Ryker grinned.

Marco breathed out a sigh. "I'm so grateful."

Zeke waved a hand. "It's what we do. This is just another way."

Ryker's cell rang and he excused himself to answer it. The conversation went to pack members. James and Sarah were moving to Mills River, and they were getting two omegas from Florida. They had applications from another three shifter families, all of them with omega pups. Marco understood their reputation as a safe space for omegas was getting around, but the adults were all bringing skills and support with them. One was a carpenter and another apparently had experience running a small farm. Dinah kept a few chickens, but they really needed to become more self-sustaining and the new land that Zeke had gotten them to the west would be perfect for animal grazing.

Ryker sat down and looked at them all expectantly which was an effective silencing technique. "I need some opinions," Ryker scratched his beard. All of them glanced at their alpha. "There's been a pack takeover in Columbia that the council just called me about."

"Columbia?" Red repeated. "But that's in Mississippi isn't it. Miles away."

"Our reputation is getting around," Ryker said dryly.

"What's happened?" Marco asked. They turned as the door opened and Emmett came in followed by Kai.

"I thought we all needed to hear this." Ryker held out a hand and Emmett rushed over. Kai immediately came over to Marco.

"Dinah's got Maddox." Marco rewarded him with a kiss. Kai was managing to leave Maddox in trusted situations for short periods of time.

"Hear what?" Emmett asked. "Dinah just said you needed us."

"The council has just called me," Ryker said. "We have a situation similar to Mills River. Omegas and pups kept in a separate bunkhouse." Ryker heaved a breath. "The enforcers started a shooting match with another other pack after a challenge. The alpha and seventeen enforcers from both sides are dead."

"Shooting?" Emmett said blankly.

Ryker met his gaze. "We also have four dead omegas who were in the way of the bullets." Kai hissed in a breath and covered his mouth with his hand. "Two deliberate shootings. I think it was a case of if we can't have them no one can."

"Oh god." Emmett teared up.

"How many are we talking about?" Chrissy asked. "And omegas or pups?"

"The omegas alive have been matched to their pups, and are going to a pack in Tennessee along with a few families that wanted to relocate. We have four pups and three bear shifter cubs unclaimed. After we've discussed things, I'm going to involve Jesse." Which made sense as Jesse was a bear shifter and he and Seth had a cub of their own.

"Unclaimed sounds like some sort of bargain basement shopping experience," Chrissy said in disgust. "These are children."

"The issue is that three packs want them because of the low birth rates, including mixed packs who aren't fussy about bears or wolves. All three packs don't have a good reputation with omegas, so the council wants us to take them until they are older and are capable of making a choice."

"Wow," Kai exclaimed. "Since when does the council interfere?"

"Since both packs used guns and it brought out the local sheriffs. This is going to take a lot of covering up." He glanced at Emmett. "This is a lot."

"Of course we'll take them," Emmett said softly and glanced at Kai. Kai nodded fiercely and Marco was immensely proud of them both. Between Emmett and Kai, they had fallen into a routine. The omegas they took in were often traumatized and being with other omegas rather than alphas seemed to settle them much more quickly.

"We need to arrange somewhere for them to be together if they already know one another. What ages?" Emmett asked.

"Between two and nine," Ryker said. "Older and they'd be taken in as gammas."

"So, we don't know if they shift or not?" Kai asked. "Not that it matters," he added.

"No." Ryker stood. "The council has offered funds for this, so we have no need to bother our benefactor." He shot a half-amused look at Zeke.

"Not that Dad would say no," Emmett replied.

"I am here," Zeke said mildly, but he shot Emmett a loving glance.

"Of course not," Ryker agreed. "But the council being indebted to us is definitely a position we want to be in." He looked at Marco and Marco understood immediately. If they were going to have any problems with his mother, they needed the council's support. Ryker glanced at Emmett and Kai. "So I can leave the logistics to you?"

"Absolutely," Kai agreed. The meeting broke up and Ryker promised to find out when they would be arriving. Ryker and Red both left and Zeke followed Ryker. "I think we need an add-on building,"

Emmett nodded. "We need a pups only space," he agreed. "Like a dorm with private spaces but somewhere for them to hang out where it's safe."

"And we need a pack mother or someone to stay in with them all the time," Kai said. "Like a human foster family almost."

"Especially if they're used to being together," Marco agreed.

Kai linked his hands with Marco as Emmett stood up. "I'm going to visit with my dad before he disappears again." He grinned and left them to it, closing the door behind him.

Marco—never one to let an opportunity slip by—clasped Kai and pulled him onto his lap. Kai immediately turned to him and buried his face in Marco's neck. Marco rubbed his back soothingly. They were both silent for a few minutes until Marco felt Kai take a breath and then he looked up.

"I didn't do it on purpose. You have to know that."

Marco arched an eyebrow. "You didn't do what?"

"Get pregnant. I mean, that's if I am, if *we* are I mean. I could be wrong. My heats are way out of whack and I was never sick with Maddox, and I'm not sick in the morning, so I could easily have just gone off coffee and—"

Marco stopped listening. Fastening his lips on Kai's suddenly seemed way more important. Kai obviously agreed as he sank into him with a happy sigh and wound his arms around Marco's neck. They were silent for a good few minutes and Marco contemplated taking Kai to their room. Kai broke off for air and cuddled in closer if that was even possible.

"I wondered if you were going to tell me or just wait until you went into labor."

Kai did the same "o" with his mouth that Maddox did, then he thumped him on the arm.

"Ow," Marco grinned.

"You knew?" Kai asked indignantly.

Marco chuckled. "I'm pretty sure I'm the last of your friends to know if it helps."

Kai looked horrified. "But I haven't told anyone." Marco smothered a laugh.

"So, Dinah suddenly never offering you coffee and practically standing over you while you eat wasn't a clue?" Kai flushed. "And while I love it, haven't you noticed that if I ever miss any other of Maddox's feedings, I don't miss his evening one?"

Kai punched him again, but a smile quirked his lips. Then he paused. "Wait. Is that why Emmett kept going on about converting the spare room next to ours to make the suite bigger in case Maddox needed a playroom?"

Marco threw back his head and laughed. He hadn't known about that.

"I thought that was weird because we need every inch of space we have at the moment in the main house, especially with the new pups on their way."

Marco hugged him tight. "I love you so damned much."

Kai froze and raised his eyes. They were silent for a moment while they just drank each other in.

"You love me?" Kai whispered breathlessly.

Marco smiled lazily. "Of course I do. I just didn't want to put any pressure on you by telling you."

Kai growled. A cute totally omega I'm-going-to-defy-nature-and-shift-just-because-I'm-mad-growl, and the sound went right to Marco's heart, lodged there, and made it it's home.

"I love you right back," Kai admitted, which of course got him another kiss. "I was worried you might feel trapped or something."

Marco scoffed. "Are you kidding me? I'm right where I want to be." He brushed Kai's lips again, then leaned back, smiling. It was perfect.

The door opened and Chrissy rushed in. "We just heard the pups are on their way."

Kai jumped off Marco's lap. "*Now?*"

"But we only found out about them twenty minutes ago," Marco protested and they both followed Chrissy into the kitchen.

It was crazy. Kai grabbed Josie to leave Emmett's hands free. Darriel had ahold of Maddox and both his girls were asleep in their double stroller, so Kai went to sit with him. Marco shot him a grateful glance. Ryker was on the phone and suddenly swore.

"Where?"

Everyone fell silent at Ryker's tone. Marco's heart beat a warning. He turned to Jack who was just grabbing a juice. "Go to the clinic and fetch me the large black bag." Jack immediately sped off. Everyone stared at Ryker. "We'll be fifteen minutes. Call Mills River." He stuffed his phone in his pocket and looked up.

"The bus carrying the pups has overturned on the road just below Lawson's Corner. There're multiple bumps and bruises, but they're all shifters and no one's critical. The ranger service managed to get it directed to us. Human authorities are unaware, but we have to be quick as hunters use that road."

Marco took his bag from Jack and sent him running for some extras. He glanced at Kai.

Go, Kai mouthed. "We'll have everything set up when you get back."

Chrissy was already outside with the second truck and Red fastened baby seats in it.

"I can get the helicopter." Zeke offered, but Ryker shook his head.

"Nowhere to land. How the hell they got a bus up that pass is beyond me. No one uses that to get here."

Which was true Marco thought. The main road was deliberately kept unattractive to deter humans, but Lawson's Corner was barely a track. Whoever was driving that bus must have been crazy.

With a brief kiss to Kai's upturned mouth, Marco followed Ryker out to the truck. "What else do we know?"

Ryker pulled out his phone. "I'm trying to get ahold of one of our guys from the ranger service but they're short today. They had a report of a possible bear attack and a separate one of a climber who failed to check in. The only ones available at the moment are humans that don't know us."

"Who called it in?"

"The council contact got a message from the driver. He says he thinks everyone's okay, but he sounded overwhelmed." Ryker scowled. "I can't find out how many adults are with them."

"It sounds like a complete shit show," Red commented.

"Yeah, as if the pups haven't been through enough," Marco agreed. Marco looked behind him. Chrissy and Fox were in the eight-seater truck complete with a couple of baby seats. Marco hung onto the grab bar as Ryker bounced through a couple of deep ruts.

Red turned around from where he sat next to Ryker. "Kai looked happy. You both all sorted now?" Marco grinned. Ryker chuckled.

"We'll take that as a yes."

He just had to get his sister to fourteen safely, then Regina would take over, or possibly even Nicholas.

Nicholas had called him twice after he had let him know he had another number. Once about two days after he had seen him and the second time a week later, sounding more frantic each time. Marco felt like shit, but he couldn't tell Nicholas that he knew where Trina was. Hopefully Nicholas would understand and forgive him when he found out she was safe.

Maybe he wouldn't.

Marco was jerked out of his thoughts when they hit another particular crappy bit of road. It took twenty minutes before they neared Lawson's Corner. "Just around this bend," Ryker said and slowed carefully, then Marco leaned forward in disbelief. The minibus—because that's what it was—was tilted into the ditch, and the nearest tire was in pieces. There was a large man—he would guess he was the driver—leaning against the hood, smoking. An older woman was trying to corral what looked like four kids and one older child was trying to comfort two smaller ones.

"Fuck," Marco swore and Ryker echoed him, but all of them, including Chrissy and Fox, filed out of the trucks. Marco went for the nearest crying child and hunkered down. He saw the tell-tale immediate inhale of the little boy but knew he wouldn't smell a shifter. He opened his arms anyway and the little scrap obviously decided he didn't care and flung himself into Marco's arms sobbing almost uncontrollably. He stood with him easily balanced, his head tucked under his chin and strode to where Ryker just about had the driver up against the bus by his throat.

"Alpha," Marco said sternly to get his attention and Ryker growled and let go. The driver scrambled back out of the way. The older woman approached them timidly trying to hold three different pairs of hands that were grabbing for her. "I'm Ryker, Alpha of the Blue Ridge Mountain pack—"

"Shifter Rescue," she interrupted in a whisper and tears ran down her face. Chrissy rushed over and handed Ryker the little girl she had and took the older woman in her arms. Ryker didn't seem disturbed at the alteration and kissed the little one's head. Marco smiled as she tightened her arms around his neck. She didn't know or didn't care what Ryker's name was, her animal recognized a powerful alpha and she knew she was safe. The boy Marco held had simply dropped asleep, probably of exhaustion, and Marco took a quick look around.

"Is anyone actually injured?"

The older woman sniffed and shook her head, seeming to pull herself together. He glanced at Chrissy. "Let's get the kids loaded up." Everyone helped. The older woman—Pamela—went back into the bus to get a couple of blankets they had brought. Marco glanced back to the driver and did a double take because he seemed to have disappeared, and something cold coiled its way up his back.

"Where is he?"

Ryker looked up and inhaled. Red did exactly the same, but with this many kids in a small space it was impossible. Marco jogged over to the bus to help Pamela.

It was empty.

"Ryker?" Marco called warningly his cat springing to alert in his head just as Ryker swung around to the trees and shouted to Red. Something was—*fuck*. Marco swore to himself as approximately fifteen enforcers stepped out of the trees, all holding rifles.

And Harker was leading them.

Chapter Eighteen

"So...," Kai said slowly to Darriel, Josie balanced in his arms as he raised his usually bare feet. Darriel had Maddox on his knee and Maddox was grabbing one of the plastic rings he liked to hold. Both the twins were asleep in their fancy newborn twin stroller that Zeke had appeared with the day after their birth. Emmett was ordering supplies to be taken to different bedrooms like some army general. "Will my ankles swell then?"

Darriel glanced over, amusement in his eyes. "So long as your head doesn't."

Kai did the second impression of a guppy that day. "You knew."

"Not for certain, but you are reacting to things you didn't used to." He bumped him with his shoulder. "I mean, refusing Dinah's hot chocolate like it was radioactive? Either you're certifiably insane or pregnant." Darriel seemed to ponder that for a moment. "Or both," he allowed, then cracked up as Kai pulled a face. Kai grinned back.

"Your alpha looked very happy about it," Darriel said softly. For a second Kai thought Darriel meant Ryker, but then he realized he was talking about Marco and knew he was correct in calling him that. Not that clans had alphas, but Marco had a quiet, dependable strength and certainly wasn't frightened of making tough decisions. Just because he had chosen to submit to Ryker didn't change his personality. Kai looked around the empty kitchen and smiled happily. He knew Emmett and Ryker loved having their own cabin, but Kai was very happy in the pack house. He felt safe and living with others was something he was used to.

"Where did you live before Mills River?" Kai asked curiously.

"Cascade Pack. It's north of Huntingdon, but I don't really remember it. I was eight when mom moved us south."

"Was Cascade Pack bad?"

Darriel shook his head and glanced inquiringly at the baby seat and to a sleeping Maddox. Kai nodded and decided to do the same with Josie so they could both get a drink. He pulled over a foot stool and helped Darriel get his feet up. "Thanks, mom," Darriel teased, but he looked relieved to be resting. Even with help, twins were hard work.

"Why did she leave then?"

"As far as I can make out, Mills River was making attractive noises about incentives for female omegas. Better living conditions. Cascade was poor and I think Mom thought we'd have a better chance at Mills River. They had a lot of land and a large pack, but the same problem with a low birth rate. She obviously didn't know what they did with male omegas."

"Do you think she knew you were one?"

Darriel sighed. "She was a birth mother, so she thought her skills would be useful in another pack. They separated us the day after we arrived."

Kai reached over and took Darriel's hand. "I'm sorry." He wished he hadn't started this conversation. Darriel squeezed it back.

"I was fourteen when I was given something to bring on a heat. I had four pregnancies, but I bled so much after I lost each one the birth mother that saw us said the alpha had to leave me alone in between or it would keep happening." He shrugged. "I have no idea if that's true, but I was glad of the respite at first, but then Riggs decided he was going to use me as his personal fuck toy each time I successfully got pregnant." Darriel sighed. "I'm so glad he's dead."

"Me too," Kai said. He hadn't known him personally, but Emmett had told him plenty, including how once the omegas got pregnant by the alpha the betas treated them like it was open season. The sick justification was that once the alpha had gotten them pregnant there wasn't any danger one of the others could. It hadn't worked like that, though.

"Do you care what you have?" Darriel asked and Kai's hand flew to his belly.

"Do you know, I've been so busy worrying about Marco's reaction I've not actually given a thought to the pup." Darriel smiled.

"Or a cat? Kitten?" Darriel teased.

Kai blinked. He hadn't thought about that either and Darriel yawned. "Maybe you need some more bed rest and someone willing to read stories to you." Kai wriggled his eyebrows.

Darriel bit his lip. "He hasn't spoken to me at all today. He came to bring the stroller, but we weren't alone and as soon as he'd seen the girls he left. I've seen him a couple of times since they were born but never on his own. He's avoiding me," Darriel added quietly.

"Emmett doesn't think it's because of his mom. Zeke thinks he's too old."

Darriel sighed. "Emmett kind of hinted that. I know it's hard for him because he feels like he's in the middle of us."

"Maybe we need to find a way you can get some time to talk?"

Darriel shook his head. "But why? Even if he thinks he's not too old for me, he still wouldn't be interested. He's a billionaire. Runs I don't know how many businesses. You should hear the stuff he knows."

"And why should that make a difference? A mate—"

"But he's human," Darriel interrupted. "Humans don't have mating instincts like shifters." He yawned again.

Kai didn't know what to say to that. Maybe Emmett could orchestrate something? He was good at that sort of thing. "Why don't you go take a nap? We have no idea how long they will be and the girls are asleep."

Darriel nodded gratefully and got to his feet, pushing the stroller with him. Kai glanced down at Josie and Maddox and thanked whoever had gifted him with an easy baby. He stood up and went over to the kitchen area and started pulling out things for sandwiches, buttering bread, and slapping them together. He had no doubt the kids would be hungry when they got back, and he could see both babies from where he was. He glanced at the clock and yawned. He was surprised they weren't back already. He hoped that didn't mean they were having problems. He heard hurried voices as Dinah and Emmett rushed back into the kitchen, Emmett holding his phone. Kai smiled, eager to hear when Marco would be back, but then he looked up and met Emmett's eyes.

And the bottom dropped out of his world.

Kai could hear the buzzing of a lot of talking, but he couldn't seem to make sense of any of it. "Kai, *Kai*," Emmett said again for his attention. "He'll be okay. You know Ryker and the others will get him back."

Kai focused on Emmett. "Tell me again what happened." Maddox was in the sling. His first instinct had been to grab him. Dinah had Josie.

"Ryker thinks it was a setup. Both the driver and the she-wolf vanished just before Harker and the enforcers appeared. The kids needing to be rehomed was genuine, but somehow someone talked and Harker found out. It could easily be bribery and just involving the driver which is why they came into that spot. Ryker says our rangers were also pulled away on false calls so there would be no one there except our guys."

"But why Marco?" But he knew. Emmett didn't answer because he knew Kai was asking a rhetorical question. "What did Harker say?"

"I don't know exactly. They just aimed their guns at everyone and told Marco to give the little boy he was holding to Chrissy. They marched him away, back into the trees."

Kai was going to ask why Ryker and the others didn't follow them when they heard the sound of engines. There seemed to be a lot of crying children, but Kai was almost numb to it. As if by rote, he grabbed the hand of the nearest little boy as Chrissy unfastened him from the seat. He was glad he had something to do and helped to usher them all into the kitchen. He turned and Ryker blocked him. "We're going back out. We just had to get the kids—"

Kai put a hand up. He couldn't talk about it, especially to his alpha, but Ryker cupped his chin and made him look. "We're going to find him."

Kai nodded because he couldn't say anything else. If he opened his mouth, he wasn't sure what would come out. Kai steered the little boy to a seat at one of the benches. Dinah had gotten out milk, juice and all the sandwiches Kai had made. "Are you hungry?"

The little boy didn't answer and Kai was forced to look at him properly. He was small for a shifter, possibly an omega but maybe just undernourished. Blond hair that looked like it had recently been hacked at by someone with a knife. He had a bruise on his cheek and another two on his arm that were yellowing. If Kai looked closely, he was sure he could see the imprint of a hand and could imagine how the bruise had happened. "What's your name?"

"Luca."

Kai squeezed his hand. "I'm Kai."

"Why do you have a baby?"

"Because he's mine." Kai took a breath and did his best to keep his voice even. "His name's Maddox."

Luca gazed up at Kai seeming to consider that, but he still didn't seem to want to sit at the table with the others. "You smell like him."

"Well, he spends a lot of time in the sling next to me, so—"

"No, the man. The one who had to go with the gammas."

Kai froze, swallowed heavily. He sat abruptly on the bench and Luca came closer. "Why did he have to go?" Kai pulled Luca into his side and did his best not to cry. If he started, he wasn't sure he could stop.

"Because he needed to make sure you were all safe."

"Hi." They both looked over at Emmett. "My name's Emmett." Luca almost cringed against Kai and Kai automatically tightened his hold. "Would you like some milk, buddy?"

"Luca," Kai prompted when it seemed like he wouldn't answer. Luca looked at the table, then shook his head and buried it in Kai's shoulder.

"Juice?" Emmett suggested being careful not to come any closer. Luca didn't answer just pressed his head in further. Emmett bit his lip.

"Luca? How about you sit with me over there?"

Luca raised his head and saw the corner with the few small tables and the cozy chairs Emmett, Kai and Darriel used to hang out in. He nodded

148

his head and immediately slipped his hand into Kai's. Kai stood up, supporting Maddox as he did so and they both went over to the corner. "Milk or juice, Luca?"

"Milk, please," he whispered as if he was frightened to answer. Emmett heard him and walked away, getting a plate together and a huge glass of milk which he came back with. Luca stared openmouthed at the plate.

"Go on," Kai said. "It's all for you, eat what you want." He'd seen the cookies and he didn't care what the little scrap ate tonight. If he wanted a cookie, he could damn well have a cookie. Kai even managed an encouraging smile when Luca reached out a shaky hand for the beef sandwich nearest to him. Footsteps made him look up. It was Ryker. He sat down, smiled at Luca and focused on Kai.

"It was a setup, did Emmett explain?"

"Is—" Kai cleared his throat. "Is this just Harker or do you think he's working with someone else?" Ryker glanced at Luca probably thinking Kai didn't want to mention Marco's mother in front of him when in reality it was he that couldn't bear to say the name. As if he spoke it, it would be true. Not that Harker wasn't bad enough.

"Emmett's calling his gran." Which answered the question. "But Trina is safe."

"What did Harker say?"

"Nothing much," Ryker bit off furiously. "Just said that M—" He glanced at Luca. "Just said that he had cost him a lot of money."

"And?" Kai whispered knowing there was more, but Ryker shook his head.

"We're going out again. We have wolves coming from Mills River to guard the compound. I'm not taking any chances."

"But you can't fight guns," Kai whispered. He bent and pressed his lips to Maddox's head for comfort. This was his fault. Harker wouldn't forgive Marco for making him look like a fool. Ryker stood. "We're going to shift. Chrissy will stay by the truck and the phone. Liam and TJ are meeting us there."

Kai met his gaze. He wanted to say so much, but he couldn't force the words out. "I need you to help Dinah and Emmett." Ryker looked down and smiled. "But I think you've got your hands full." Kai looked down. Most of his lap was covered by the sling, but Luca had still managed to find just enough room to lay his head. He was fast asleep. Kai looked back up, but Ryker had his arms around Emmett. Another minute and he was out the door followed by Chrissy, Red, and Fox.

Emmett sat down next to him. He didn't mention Marco, just bumped shoulders. Emmett didn't have to say anything, Kai knew what he meant. "What do we need to do?"

Emmett took a breath and started counting off on his fingers. "Seven kids. Luca is the youngest at four and a half. Maisie is six. The oldest is Blue at nine. The others Raine, Kelly, Daniel, and Mo don't actually know how old they are, or won't tell me. Mo and Daniel haven't said a word. Blue says they were all kept together and they're definitely younger than twelve because that's when they start training to be gammas. He says none of them have shifted yet. The ones who shift get to live with family groups, but until then they're all kept together. Mothers are never kept with their own kids."

"What about omegas?"

"The alpha wouldn't keep male omegas. As soon as that was established, they were sold." Kai met Emmett's gaze. He knew Emmett was keeping his temper for the sake of the kids, and he returned the shoulder nudge of a moment ago.

"What can I do?"

The quiet voice silenced them both and Kai stared open-mouthed at Charles. He was upright, dressed, and leaning heavily on a cane. "Should you be out of bed?" Kai exclaimed.

Charles nodded. "I think so." He looked at Emmett. "What can I do alpha-mate?"

And that quiet, formal question seemed to galvanize everyone. Kai agreed to go back to his room with Luca and Maddox. Emmett said there was room with Calvin for Daniel and Mo. Charles said he would take Blue, the oldest boy, as he didn't have the strength to carry one of them. Dinah had already taken all three girls. It would do for tonight. Sam appeared— obviously asked to—and gently picked up Luca. Kai, Charles and Blue followed him. There were other omegas running to and fro, distributing clothes, bedding, towels and air mattresses. They had empty rooms, but Emmett didn't want the kids on their own and Kai agreed. Luca came blearily awake when Sam was carrying him and panicked. Kai kept him calm by holding his hand.

He liked Blue already. Charles had stumbled and Blue had automatically reached out for him. Now he was walking very close beside him, almost protectively, and Kai decided to think about that later. They needed someone to stay with the children on a long-term basis. Charles needed a reason to live.

He was deliberately not thinking about the other thing because he would fall apart. And he couldn't do that just now.

He had to believe they would find him. He had to.

Chapter Nineteen

Marco doubled over as far as the chains would let him and spat blood from his mouth. He had a tight steel band around his neck. He'd been joyously informed by Harker that it wouldn't snap if he shifted. Harker sounded like he wished he would try and after the fuck-knew-how-many hours they'd been beating him, he was tempted.

The only thing that stopped him was Kai. Kai and both their pups, because Maddox was every bit his as their future one. He had a brief image of Kai with a round and swollen belly and was determined not to miss it. Somehow, he had to get back to them. *If Harker doesn't kill me first.*

The pain in his head was crippling, and the urge to shift and stop the pain of that alone was nearly overpowering. If he could get his hands free, he might be able to snap the collar, but he doubted he could do it with one hand. His cat prowled in anger, wanting out, but Marco knew he couldn't assume Harker was bluffing.

Harker snarled and lifted Marco's head up by the hair, but his eyes were so swollen he could barely see him. "You picked on the wrong wolf, cat." He spat and Marco barely felt the hit of saliva mixed in with so many other hurts.

Harker smiled. "Course we're going to get rid of your pathetic band for good soon. What do you think of that, huh? Shall I keep you alive long enough for you to see that fucking omega back in his place? Samson can't wait to get his property back, but this time we're going to see how long we can keep him on the good stuff. Samson says he can go at least a few days, but I'm thinking weeks with a couple of days off in between."

Where Marco found the strength to lunge at him, he didn't know, but he heard the very satisfying crack as his head connected with Harker's nose. He didn't hear much else though. Harker's punch to his jaw took care of that.

Ryker shifted back and accepted some water from Chrissy. Behind him, Red and Fox did the same.

"The scent disappears a mile back."

"Vehicle," Red confirmed taking a swig of his own water. "Multiple vehicles and there are so many wolf scents I can't get an individual read on anything." Ryker was having the same trouble although they'd all seen Harker, so they knew who was behind it.

"I don't understand how Harker thought he could get away with this. He knows Regina and the council won't free him a second time." Not that they would get the chance. Ryker would deal with Harker himself this time. He wouldn't risk another threat to any of his pack.

"What if—" But Chrissy snapped her mouth shut as they all smelled wolf. They swung around and Ryker shifted automatically and lunged before he'd even thought about it. The woman who stepped from the trees in human form barely had a chance to put her hands in front of herself protectively before he landed and she went down. Ryker had a second to recognize her before the other three caught up to him and he moved away.

"Well, well," Chrissy said menacingly. "If it isn't Pamela. Come to sell us another sob story?"

She was shaking, crying, curled almost in a fetal position and Ryker didn't doubt her fear. His wolf had been a couple of seconds from tearing out her throat. The jury was still out as far as he was concerned, even though she was clearly an omega. He shifted back. "Why are you here?"

She lowered her shaking hands. "B-because I can't get back. I haven't any money."

Ryker frowned and Chrissy scoffed again. "You left. You could have come with us the first time."

She tried to hold back her sobs. "He said he would kill me."

Ryker glanced at Chrissy briefly before looking back at Pamela. "Who?"

"Terry. He's one of the Alpha's enforcers. I didn't know what he was going to do. I swear." She wiped a hand over her face. Ryker held out a hand to her and after another few seconds she clasped it and he pulled her up.

"Who's your alpha?"

"Will Leroy. My pack's just north of Alexandria. We heard about the challenge, but my alpha wasn't involved. We wanted pups and we'd arrived to collect two, but we got a message saying the council were refusing to let them go. Said we have to bring them to you."

"Then what happened?"

"I was in the back with the babies. We weren't sent enough food for them and they were hungry, but Terry wouldn't stop. We were going up this track and then Terry suddenly swerved and ran us into the ditch. "I couldn't hear what was being said over the crying, but he just gets out all casual like and says someone's coming to help."

"And then?" Chrissy prompted.

"Then Terry told me I had to do exactly as he said or else. That as soon as he gave the signal I needed to run because what had happened in Columbia was a cake walk compared to what was coming. He said someone was on their way for the kids, but I wasn't to go with them. I could go back to my pack." Ryker sighed to himself. "Anyway, you guys came, and Terry looked at me, so I made the excuse about the blankets and ran after him."

"Why are you still here?"

Fresh tears ran down her face but either she wasn't aware of them or didn't care. "Terry met up with an alpha and some enforcers." She swallowed. "They had guns. And the alpha—I think he was the alpha—laughed when he saw me and said...said he wasn't that desperate, and they got in the cars and drove off."

Ryker met Chrissy's eyes.

"Did you see anyone with them being forced to go?" Red asked.

She nodded. "But he wasn't a wolf I don't think. He was being marched between two of them because they were having to hold him up. I think one of them had hit him. He had blood." She pointed to her forehead and Red glanced at Ryker.

"Do you think they'll take Marco back to—"

"That was Marco?" Pamela interrupted wide-eyed.

Every hair on the back of Ryker's neck stood up. "How do you know the name?"

"Because we stopped just outside of Tuscaloosa and picked up another wolf I'd never seen before. We dropped him off about an hour back before we started climbing the road. He and Terry were talking and he was saying he had a job. I heard him mention the name Marco a few times. Said there were a lot of people wanting him out of the way."

Ryker didn't look at the other two as a chill ran up his spine. Was there a chance Harker wasn't acting on his own? That Marco's mother had found a way to get someone else to do her dirty work for her?

"You'd better come with us," Ryker said. They needed to regroup. Call Regina. They could shift and go for Harker if they could find him, but three wolves couldn't do fuck all against more than a dozen enforcers with guns.

She shook her head and took a step back. "I have a sister back home and I help with the pack cubs. Even if I can't shift, they're good to me. I want to go home." She clearly didn't trust them.

"We can't just leave you."

"And I'm not coming with you," she said implacably.

"I can send someone back down with a car, but we have to go get our friend."

"I'll make sure she gets down there safely and gets a ride," Fox said. "I'll call when I'm done, and you can pick me up."

Ryker frowned. He didn't like leaving her, especially since she couldn't shift. He glanced at Chrissy. "Give her some clothes, a phone and some cash."

Pamela looked relieved and took the things Chrissy passed her. She looked up at Ryker, nodded once, then turned and walked into the trees. Fox right behind her.

Ryker threw Chrissy the keys and he climbed into the back of the truck to pull on his spare clothes. Then he dialed Regina. And hoped with everything in him that it wasn't already too late.

Kai fed Maddox and true to form he settled down almost instantly. Luca was awake and hungry again, so Kai sent him into the shower, then helped him wash his hair. Isabelle arrived with food and some clothes that should fit Luca. The filthy shorts and T-shirt he had been wearing needed to be burned. Luca managed to stay awake long enough to eat everything and then, instead of making him sleep on the air mattress, Kai just tucked him into bed next to him. It was early, but the little guy was completely exhausted. In another few minutes there was a soft knock at the door and Dinah came in. "Ryker's on his way back. I'll stay in here while you go see what's happening."

He stood up, glad he hadn't gotten undressed and shot to the door. Dinah patted his arm. "He'll be fine," she promised. Kai smiled because she seemed to expect he would agree and jogged back to the kitchen.

Emmett was there and looked up as Kai rushed in. "Ryker's talking to my gran. They have news and we need to make some decisions." Kai nodded even though there was only one decision to make as far as he was concerned.

"Sit down," Emmett fussed, and Kai sat automatically, still working on auto pilot. In another moment a bottle of water was in front of him. "I didn't think you'd appreciate milk or coffee," Emmett said gently. Kai knew Emmett had guessed he was pregnant, but that wasn't something he could think about just now. He had to focus on Marco.

The guys all arrived around thirty minutes later. Sam joined them along with three younger gammas who weren't on the rescue squad. Ryker hugged Emmett and sat, launching into an explanation of everything they knew, how they'd found out and where Fox was.

"I'm waiting for Regina to call back. The trouble is, I don't want to waste a full seven hours going to Harker's pack if he isn't there. We need to know where to look to find him and we could easily be going in the opposite direction."

"But we might never know," Kai whispered, but he knew everyone had heard him. Ryker inclined his head.

"If we don't get any information from Regina, we go anyway. Jered and fifteen enforcers are on their way from Mills River because this is sanctioned by the council. I wish I could say the council is finally doing the right thing because they had a change of heart, but the real issue is the guns. Anything that draws unwanted human attention is frowned upon, so we have their blessing to resolve this in any way I see fit, including a challenge."

Emmett's indrawn hiss was the only noise in the room and for the first time another fear clutched hold of Kai. He'd seen how fast Harker was. Being responsible for getting Marco hurt was bad enough, but Ryker as well?

Nausea washed over Kai, and he bolted from the room, just making it to the nearest bathroom in time. He'd locked the door and as he rinsed his mouth, he heard Chrissy calling him from the other side.

"I just need a minute," he croaked. "I'll come back."

"You sure?"

"Yes. Give me a couple of minutes." He heard the sound of her feet retreating and slid down the wall to the floor, putting his hands across his belly. He didn't know what to do. His instinct was to rush out and find Marco himself, but there wasn't just him to consider. Marco's baby was in there and he had to protect him or her as much as he had Maddox. He banged his head back on the tiled wall in frustration and ignored the buzz from the phone in his pocket. It was probably Emmett, and he wasn't sure he could face him right now with what he was asking Ryker to risk.

It buzzed again and he pulled it out just in case it was Dinah because

Maddox was awake, and frowned at the unknown number and read the text:

Marco gave me this no. I'm Nicholas, Marco's bro. I promised I'd only use it if it was a 911. Pls call me. Worried. Vital u r on own 2 talk.

Kai's heart thudded and he pressed the call button immediately.

A gruff voice sounding so much like Marco answered immediately. "Kai?"

Kai gripped the phone tighter. "Yes."

He heard the audible noise of relief. "Are you on your own?"

"Yes."

"This is important. Do you know who our mother is?" He nodded, then realized Nicholas couldn't see him.

"The Panthera."

"Yes, and she just got a call from a wolf alpha named Harker." Kai hissed in a breath then clamped his lips together as his stomach roiled. This was a nightmare. With enough firepower they could take on Harker, but the Panthera leader or whatever she was on the west coast? Not a chance in hell. And he honestly wasn't sure how far Regina could go as it wasn't her geographical area and clans had all sorts of bullshit rules.

"I take it he has him?" Nicholas sounded resigned. Kai quickly gave him a run down of what had happened.

Nicholas was silent for a moment. "I have an idea, but this has to just involve you. The wolves will get nowhere near where he's being kept. He has panther shifters there already, and they wouldn't hesitate to use force."

Kai closed his eyes in horror. "But what can I do?"

"He's convinced the Panthera wants Marco, but she isn't interested. He's dead to her and she's certainly not going to pay any money to get him back. Harker lost face which hit him hard and he's decided that getting in with the Panthera would keep the council off his back, or it would have been if Mother agreed."

It was on the tip of Kai's tongue to tell him his other problem when Nicholas carried on. "I managed to talk to him. I told him Mother had to abide by the council rules, but that I would come and get him, pay for him.

But Harker said no. He's insisting the Panthera come herself which isn't going to happen, so we're at an impasse."

Kai still wasn't seeing a solution.

"This is where you can help. Samson wants you back. It looks bad for Harker because he let an omega slip through his fingers. Couple that with mating Marco and you're a huge target. I can contact Harker and offer to deliver you so long as he accepts that he'll just meet me and not the Panthera. I think it's enough of an incentive to make him agree. Don't worry, you will both be perfectly safe. I won't let anything happen to either you or Marco. She can't do anything openly and this way she can leak out that the whole rescue was her idea. She'll have the council in the palm of her hand when it's sorted tidily with no human involvement, and you two can just go home."

"But you said he has all those enforcers and panthers."

Nicholas scoffed. "He hasn't met the claw. Have you ever seen the size of Marco fully shifted? They don't stand a chance, but I have to get in there, and the only way I can do that is by promising to deliver you."

Kai looked down at his belly and splayed his hand over it. He had to keep his little one safe, but this seemed to be their only option. "What do you want me to do?"

"I need you to sneak out."

Kai frowned. "I don't see how that's possible. We've got the claw protecting the pack house and Mills River is on their way to go with Ryker."

"Which means everyone will be distracted just as Mills River arrives and they load up. That's your chance. I can meet you wherever you say. I'm close."

"There's a clearing," and he described the area Emmett had told him about.

"Too far when you can't shift." Which was true.

"Do you know the pack house?"

"Only from what Marco told me."

"There's a small cabin," Kai told Nicholas. "It's on the far eastern side. It used to be the alpha's, but its empty because it can't be seen from the main house and they don't think it's safe. There's a track that runs close to the back that leads to the road. I'll be there as soon as they're all distracted."

Nicholas was silent for a moment. "I'll make sure your pack goes the other way so they're safe and out of harm's way. I'm grateful. I can't lose another sibling." He choked off the last word and Kai felt like shit for keeping Trina a secret, but he'd promised. Nicholas hung up and Kai took a deep breath. He wasn't sure if this would work, but he knew Marco had put his faith in Nicholas before and if he didn't go, the pack would try and rescue him and be slaughtered.

And if they didn't get Marco out, Harker would kill him. They were running out of time.

He got up slowly and made his way back to the kitchen. Ryker stood in the corner on the phone. As soon as he appeared, Emmett rushed over to him and threw his arms around his shoulders. "This isn't your fault. You hear me?"

Kai swallowed and returned the hug. He wasn't convinced but he needed the touch. "What's happening?"

"They think they know where Marco is. Gran got some info from a panther in Marco's old clan. Apparently, something's going on and he doesn't approve. He wouldn't talk to wolves, but he made contact with her." Which is what Nicholas must have meant.

"Good," he said weakly.

Chrissy saw him and came over. "I just checked with Dinah and both your sleeping beauties are out cold." She smiled gently and Kai took an easier breath. This had to work. He helped Chrissy get the first aid things ready, although Marco hadn't used his bag so there wasn't much to do. The second the Mills River trucks pulled into the yard Ryker ended his call. "Apparently there's a meeting arranged at an old campground just outside of Bryson City, backing onto the national forest. Regina is texting me directions. The council don't want a clan war starting, so she's not authorized to come herself, but with the enforcers from Mills River we should be good."

Kai nodded, and as if he was an automaton, he followed them into the yard, pulling on a jacket as if he was going to stand and watch them go. Emmett clutched Ryker, then everyone rushed to sort out gear and receive instructions. Mills River didn't have guns, but they had huge tranquilizer rifles. The second Emmett saw them, Kai put a hand over his mouth and muffled an apology as if he was going to be sick and rushed back in the kitchen. But instead of heading for the bathroom, he went down the corridor to the storerooms and out the back door, closing it carefully behind him. He was banking on everyone concentrating on what was happening at the front and hoped the claw wouldn't be extra vigilant until after they knew Ryker had gone. He ran across the grass and into the trees, heading around to Ryker's old cabin. It took five minutes to get to the road. He immediately saw the black truck waiting and rushed over.

The door opened and a man reached over to help him up. He didn't need an introduction. He was so like Marco it almost physically hurt. "I've arranged for your pack to get sent in the opposite direction. Not too far, but enough for us to be in and out with Marco without incident. I called Harker and he's agreed to the exchange. I also told him I had my claw with me as there was no way I was seeing him without protection."

Kai curled his fingers tightly together to stop his hands from shaking. "Where are your guys meeting us?"

"They're meeting us there."

Kai didn't reply, just looked out of the window at the fading light and hoped with everything he had they were going to get there in time. And he promised himself when he got Marco home, he was never going to let him out of his sight again.

Chapter Twenty

Ryker was silent as they set off for the third time that day. He could have bitten his tongue off for mentioning the word "challenge" in front of Emmett. What had he been thinking? It was the only way he could keep his family safe, but he shouldn't have said anything in front of Emmett. Saying it in front of Kai wasn't much better, but as a wolf Kai was more likely to understand why he had to do it.

Although between Marco, fear over his pregnancy, and Maddox, Kai had enough on his plate, and he had seen a challenge go badly wrong. Ryker frowned and tried to remember Kai's reaction. He'd seemed numb which was a little understandable, but when they were loading up, he'd asked zero questions, nothing. It was likely shock after everything he'd been through, but when he had put his jacket on Ryker had half expected Kai to ask to come.

His cell phone rang. It was Regina. "I've just had a message that Marco is in Roanoke." Ryker swore and Chrissy eased her foot off the gas, looking at him in the mirror.

"That's in the opposite direction."

"Indeed," Regina confirmed.

"If it's wrong..."

Regina was silent for a moment then said, "This call came through the shifter council which should add weight to the message. It was from an unspecified shifter."

Ryker chewed the inside of his cheek. "What do you think?"

"Well, one of them is clearly wrong, but what I'd be asking myself is, how many of your wolves would know how to approach the shifter council? Because I can categorically say it is only my close inner circle that would know as far as the clan goes. The council isn't exactly approachable. Only the members that serve on it know exactly who they are or indeed how many there are. I know of two panthers, one bear and two wolves, but even I'm not sure if there are more."

"What are you saying?"

"This is your call Ryker, but if it were me, I would believe the original story. But if I'm wrong, it may cost Marco his life."

"If we were searching for Emmett where would you go?" He had already decided but wanted to know what Regina thought.

"I wouldn't be turning around," she said softly. He agreed and hung up.

"Keep heading in the original direction," he told Chrissy. He felt the truck almost leap forward and put his head back. They got a call ten minutes later to say one of the Mills River trucks had Fox with them. It had been a good idea of Fox to call them as it was quicker for one of them to divert.

"What's the plan, Alpha?" Red said immediately showing his respect by not calling Ryker by his name as he usually did, or teasing like he used to.

"What's the area like?"

"Haven Woods it's called. It shut down three years ago when they diverted the highway making the access longer. They were offered incentives to relocate which they did successfully, and the area is marked for regeneration but has stalled because of cash. There was a small store, office, swimming pool and hook ups for about thirty RVs, plus a campground."

Ryker sighed. "We can't come in stealthily, especially if he has rogue panthers, because we couldn't scent them." He pondered this. "Maybe I should go on my own and offer a challenge. He seems to be fond of those, and if I taunt him enough, I doubt he'd back down."

"With a second," Red agreed.

"It will be a setup though," Chrissy pointed out.

"Maybe," Ryker agreed, "but what I'd like to know is, why are they sending us on a wild goose chase? What is he hoping to prevent? He's not holed up there because he wants to kill Marco. I think he has more ambitious plans, which we will screw up if we arrive too early." Ryker got out his phone to study the area and to see what he could get from Google maps, but Emmett's name flashed on the screen and he answered it before it rang. "Hey. We're—"

"Kai's missing."

Ryker almost closed his eyes, and internally his wolf growled. The sound must have been audible because Chrissy slowed again. Ryker leaned forward. "Hurry." Then he turned his attention back to the phone. "How long?" And he put the phone on speaker.

"No one's seen him since you guys left. A few of us saw him go back inside, but we think he just went out the back door."

"Kai?" Red asked and Ryker nodded.

"Shit," Chrissy swore.

"And one of my gran's claw says there was a vehicle close to the back of your old cabin. It was gone when he checked, but he smelled the gas fumes after you guys had gone. It had to have been there recently."

"You think someone picked up Kai?" Red asked.

"It must have been voluntarily," Ryker said. "We'd have heard a commotion if someone tried to take him and there's no way he would have gone anywhere by himself."

Chrissy met his eyes in the mirror and Ryker sighed. "He's pregnant."

Red's eyebrows rose. "Shit."

"Which means there had to be a big incentive. He's barely let Maddox out of his sight since we got him back," Chrissy remarked.

"Marco," Ryker agreed. "Emmett, we'll be there soon. If you hear anything else, text me. The phones will all be going on silent." Emmett agreed, told him he loved him, and hung up.

Ryker thought hard, especially about what Chrissy had just said. "It makes no sense. He adores Marco, but he wouldn't risk his child. Do we really think if someone said, 'Get into this car or we'll kill Marco,' that he would? The mating instinct is a powerful thing, we all know that. But putting an unborn child at risk as well?"

"You're thinking he must have gotten into the car because he felt safe, not threatened," Chrissy said immediately catching on.

"But who?" Red asked bewildered. "Who else is there not at the pack that he would even know, let alone trust?"

Ryker tapped his phone thoughtfully, then called Regina again. When he finished, he called Zeke and suggested he go check on Trina. There was something else going on except the obvious, he was sure of it.

Marco came around slowly and with the pounding in his head immediately wished he hadn't. It took him a second to work out that he still had the collar on, but he was lying down on some sort of thin mattress which was a distinct improvement. Not that it meant his chances of getting free were any better. He heard a door open somewhere above him, then footsteps approaching. It sounded like he was underground. Maybe in some type of cellar? There were certainly no windows and some old plastic tubing had been tossed in a corner. He just caught a glimpse of what looked like a pair of child's armbands—the type you used in a swimming pool—when the footsteps stopped. Marco turned his head. By not so much as an eyebrow lift did he show any reaction to Harker or the two goons who were with him. He'd shifted because his nose hadn't a mark on it and Marco remembered he'd broken it. Harker eyed him calmly.

"You have a visitor."

Marco deliberately kept his face calm, glad again he wasn't a wolf shifter or Harker would have been able to scent his distress. "Really?" He tried to sound bored.

Harker nodded to the two wolf shifters and they pulled him up none too gently. It was only then he saw his clothes had been changed and the blood wiped off of him. His heart sank. That meant his mother was here and Harker wanted to earn brownie points with her. He almost laughed. The worst beating of his life was by her hand.

Or not hers exactly. All the punches she threw were metaphorical ones. She just stood around and watched while her claw did it. As they got him up and dragged him to the steps, he realized he was surprised. He hadn't expected her to come herself. It was risky if the council found out she knew.

In fact, it made zero sense. There was no way she would come here. He narrowed his eyes as they emerged outside briefly and tried to work out where they were. Some sort of industrial area? Was that an empty swimming pool? Where the hell were they? He followed Harker and the two wolves into the next building. Marco nearly stumbled at the scent he recognized and heard the small inhale. Heart pounding, he stared in disbelief. Kai stood next to Samson. Samson, a clearly satisfied smirk on his face, was clutching Kai so tight he couldn't move.

"Marco."

Marco swung his head at the second shock. "Nicholas?" and his heart beat harder for a different reason. If somehow Nicholas had convinced their mother he needed to come and get him, then they had a chance and hope flared in his chest. It didn't explain why Kai was here though. Marco took in the five large panther shifters standing behind Nicholas, then turned to Harker.

"Surprised?" Harker taunted. "I love a family reunion." He nodded to the wolf standing next to him and the wolf stepped forward with a set of keys. Marco realized he was going to unlock his collar and he met Kai's eyes. Doing his best to assure his gorgeous mate that everything was going to be okay.

"Actually, no, don't do that." Nicholas stepped forward.

"What?" Marco exclaimed.

Nicholas shot Marco an almost apologetic look. "I won't get him outside if you do."

Marco stilled and narrowed his eyes. What the fuck was Nicholas playing at? He glanced back at Kai and saw the terrified look on his face, the defeat and something cold slid down his spine. He stared at his brother. "What did you do?"

Nicholas frowned. "I'm getting you home. Mother ordered us back immediately." But Marco shook his head.

"I'm going nowhere without my mate."

Samson snarled. "He's mine."

Nicholas shrugged. "It's business. Mother wants you back and she's paid for the privilege." But it was a lie. His mother wouldn't pay to get him back. She'd known where he was for months. "Let's get going."

Marco tried to think around the pounding in his head. He wasn't going with Nicholas. He glanced at the panthers and the wolves. Both looking at each other with suspicion. "I'm not leaving without Kai." Even if Nicholas had a plan to get them both out, he wasn't leaving without Kai. He had to stall.

It was Harker's turn to frown. He glanced at Nicholas. "I suggest you leave. I'm not hanging around here. I have a pack to move."

"Nicholas. I can't go without Kai."

His brother glanced at him. Irritation on his face. "He's a wolf," he snapped out. "Didn't you learn your fucking lesson the last time?"

Marco jerked back as if Nicholas had hit him. He stared at his brother. That wasn't fake. That was...*resentment.* How much did his brother resent him? A different sort of unease slid over his skin and he remembered the apartment. The luxury penthouse, the designer clothes, the car. Would Nicholas really risk all that to come and get a brother he hadn't seen in nearly fifteen years? And what was supposed to happen afterwards? Did he expect Marco to just go back to the clan? It made no sense. What was supposed to happen to Harker? There was something else going on he didn't understand. Maybe they were supposed to leave and the claw would swoop in and finish them? Clean up, so to speak?

Nicholas gestured to one of the panther shifters and he moved closer to Marco, but Marco wasn't leaving without Kai. If he stepped out of this building without him, Kai was as good as dead. Either the claw would simply take everyone out, or Samson would take him. Neither one was happening. He watched again as the enforcers eyed the claw warily. He knew it wouldn't take much of a spark to set them off. It might be his only chance.

He glanced at Harker. Knew he hoped his dealing with Nicholas would get him back some power. "Let me guess? Kai was the sweetener to let my brother take me instead of the Panthera."

Harker smirked. "Well, we can't expect important ladies to—"

"Bullshit!" Marco spat out. "My mother's known where I was for months. There is zero chance she would pay money to get me." And he turned to his brother. "Does she even know?"

"What the fuck?" Harker snarled and took a threatening step forward at the same time as the panthers, but before anyone could say a word the door was flung open, and a wolf stumbled in. He crumpled to the floor just as he shifted to a wolf and the small dart that was stuck in the back of his neck fell out and rolled away.

All hell broke loose. The panthers shifted as did the wolves, but they went for each other which was what Marco was hoping for. He leaped for Kai. Bodies rushed in, immediately shifting, and Marco recognized Ryker. Ryker used both his hands to break the collar from Marco's neck before Ryker shifted and went for a wolf. Samson was so terrified he made no attempt to stop Marco as he gathered Kai in his arms.

"Marco!"

Marco whirled just in time to see a shifted wolf leaping for him, but Marco was too fast for him and they met in midair. The wolf didn't stand a chance as all. Five hundred pounds of Marco in cat form hit him and snapped his neck before they'd even landed.

Marco snarled, his panther ready to rip heads, but the sudden silence echoed loudly and he whipped around at the same time as everyone came to a stop.

Marco immediately shifted back. He was going to need words as he stared into Kai's eyes. He didn't even look at Harker who held Kai against him as a human shield, the tip of the knife Harker wielded pressing against

Kai's throat. He met Kai's eyes and for a moment it was as if there was no one else there.

"That's better," Harker rasped. "Glad I have your attention." He looked at Nicholas. "Is it true?"

Nicholas scoffed. "As if I could do anything without the express approval of the Panthera."

Harker nodded as if that was perfectly reasonable. "Call her then. And make sure it's on speaker."

Nicholas paled and that's when everyone knew he was lying. Harker snarled. "And do you have your claw waiting outside as well? Ready to tidy up your loose ends when you got out?" He laughed. "You think I wasn't ready for you? You think I would let you live for one fucking second?"

Nicholas smiled. "And what makes *you* think for one tiny second that you holding a knife to that *thing* would make me change my mind?"

Kai gave a grunt of pain as Harker almost absently pressed him closer. Marco saw the exact moment when he heard the second heartbeat and Harker's face changed. He even lowered the knife in shock, but it was just the distraction Marco needed. Marco shifted and launched himself at Harker who had to let go of Kai and shifted a second later. He was fast, but not as fast as a desperate panther shifter who would do anything—absolutely anything—to keep his mate safe. Marco took him down just as the room exploded again.

He met Harker's wolf, claws for sharp claws, fangs for fangs, 500 pounds of sheer packed muscle rolled and as his weight gained momentum, he reached down and closed his teeth around Harker's neck. Harker froze. For the first time, fear registered in his brown eyes and Marco hesitated. Harker was clever and took advantage, bringing a paw up and raking it across Marco's back. Blood spurted out, but Marco didn't even feel it.

A second later, in human form Marco staggered to his feet and pushed Harker's dead body away. He looked for Kai. Ryker was holding him, but let him go as soon as Marco was clear and Marco just had time to see Chrissy licking Samson's blood off her paws as he bled out all over the floor.

Nicholas never even looked at Marco, simply stepped over Harker's dead body and out of the door, not even waiting for the few panther shifters still in the room.

A warm, live body slammed into him and Marco closed his eyes and pressed Kai close. Utter exhilarating relief shot through him like fireworks. He clung on. And promised himself he wasn't letting go.

Not ever again.

Chapter Twenty-One

Marco kept Kai on his lap all the way back home. Ryker said he was staying to sort out the stragglers from Harker's pack and would contact the shifter council to put the whole sorry mess firmly in their hands. Fox drove Marco and Kai home right away and Mills River stayed to help Ryker and the others.

Kai sat quietly, seeming to be content with gentle weight of Marco's hand splayed protectively over his belly. "I can't wait to get you home and to start our family properly," Marco said. "Another three months and we'll have two pups." He wanted to make it a hundred percent clear to Kai that he considered Maddox his.

"Maybe three," Kai whispered.

It took Marco a minute. "You think we're having twins?"

Kai chuckled and Marco grinned because Kai was safe and everything was going to be okay. "No, or I hope not," he said in mild alarm. "I think I need to tell you there's a four-year-old pup named Luca currently asleep in our bed." Kai gazed up at him. "He said I smelled like you."

Even Fox chuckled at that, though Marco guessed he was trying not to listen. "The little one from the minibus?" Kai nodded.

Kai was silent for a moment but then asked. "What did you think of your brother?"

"Tell me what happened." Marco brushed a kiss on Kai's head and Kai told them both about Nicholas texting him, then picking him up.

"I genuinely believed he wanted to help. It seemed to be the only thing any of us could do."

"And we would have been screwed if it wasn't for Regina not believing the story about where you were," Fox said and told them both about the deliberately false information, and wondered who had given Regina the correct details.

"What was he going to do with you though?" Kai asked. "He had to know you wouldn't just walk away from me." Marco smiled and rewarded Kai with a kiss for showing such complete trust in him.

Marco knew exactly what had been going to happen. "I think Nicholas fooled me. When I went to see him, he said my other brother Nathaniel had changed and was back living with our mother—the Panthera." Marco quickly amended because she hadn't been his mother for a very long time. "But I'm not convinced that was true. Having said that, I knew she wasn't aware of what was happening with Harker. She would never have paid any money to get me back."

"So, what was the plan, then?" Fox asked.

"I don't think I was going to live. I think his claw was going to kill everyone and blame my death on collateral damage."

"But why?" Kai said. "You're not involved in the clan. And you're not female so you can't be a threat to either of them."

Something cold and hard seemed to coil in Marco's chest and he reached forward. "Can I borrow your phone?"

Fox handed it over and Marco called Zeke who answered immediately. "Is Trina okay?"

"Absolutely," Zeke confirmed immediately. "I just spoke to May and she's just aced her last paper. You have a very clever sister. In fact, I don't think online schooling is enough and I was thinking about hiring a tutor."

Marco breathed out a sigh of relief, thanked Zeke and hung up. "What is it?" Kai asked.

"You remember Regina saying Trina could be sponsored by a family member to assume her majority when she's fourteen?"

"And you're the family member," Kai said bluntly.

Marco nodded. "Somehow they might have found out Trina was on her way here."

"There was a small article about the girl that Trina found," Fox commented. "It was local. Just saying good work that sort of thing. I don't think Red mentioned it because he was embarrassed, but it could easily have been flagged by a computer set up to notice supposed panther sightings."

Marco chewed his lip. "I think we may have to move her again. I'm going to talk to Ryker and Zeke when we get back. Consult Regina."

"If we have to move, then we have to move."

Marco's eyes widened and a lump seemed to lodge in Marco's throat. He knew what Kai was saying and he drew him close. So long as they were together everything would be okay. "I love you so much."

Kai answered him with a kiss. Marco ignored the comment from the front about "getting a room."

Kai broke off for air after a while. "Oh, I forgot. I have an idea about the new pups and I think it might help Charles."

The car jerked a little as Fox's head came up so quickly to listen his hands slipped a little. Marco eyed him in amusement. It looked like someone else might be getting a mate. He hoped so.

Epilogue

Kai balefully gazed at the teething ring that Maddox had dropped and knew absolutely that his enormous baby bump wasn't about to allow him to bend down and get it. Luckily Luca spotted it and picked it up. He even handed it back to Kai so Kai could wash it before Maddox got his hands on it again. At six months old, Maddox was sitting up and just beginning to scoot along on his well-diapered butt much to the glee of his "official" older brother Luca who was just as proud of his baby brother as he was when his new bestie Calvin had invited him into the gamma cadets.

Then he read the email Marco had given him from his brother. Garth had been frantically searching for him. Had joined a really good pack in Tennessee and couldn't wait to meet him and introduce him to his two nephews and three nieces. *Wow.* Kai giggled. Garth had always been an overachiever. But he couldn't say how much it had warmed his heart to find out he had other family that wanted him. Apart from his current one of course. Because he was a million percent sure of that.

Kai wriggled his toes, glad that his ankles hadn't swollen too much and after today—maybe this afternoon—it would hopefully be a thing of the past. Marco had been called out of their warm bed a couple of hours ago as there had been a lost hiker that the rangers service had needed help with because it had been so close to their pack house. The hiker had been found with a broken ankle and a little hypothermia, but he was okay and Rescue One was on their way back.

Which was perfect timing, because Kai wouldn't have been able to hide that he was in labor if Marco was present and he needed time to set everything up.

Emmett sat down on the chair next to him and eyed him. "How are you doing?"

"About ready." The twinges across his belly were morphing into something a little stronger. He looked up at the quiet footsteps and smiled at Charles and Blue as they came into the kitchen.

"Will you be okay?" Kai asked and Charles smiled gently.

"We'll be fine. All the pups are excited about having guests for a sleepover tonight. I have games, coloring books, and even some videos set up for anyone who's still awake."

Kai reached out and clasped Charles's hand and Charles squeezed back. As Kai had predicted, moving Charles into the newly built pups' area had been a master stroke for everyone. The pups from Columbia, except Luca, were all happily ensconced in there, two to a bedroom, and they'd even just added another new teenager who had arrived last week and was sharing with Blue. Charles had his own room of course, but it had given him the new lease on life Kai had been hoping for. He was even strong enough to carry the babies and toddlers now and he didn't need his cane. It also meant that the pups had someone to call their own and Charles didn't mind what that was. The older ones called him Charles, but the first time Kai had heard one of the smaller ones call him Daddy, Kai had cried right alongside him.

Charles and Blue were taking the twins, Luca, Josie and Maddox for the rest of the day and Calvin would join them after school. The teenager Jack, plus one of the other single omegas, had also been roped in to help. Darriel and Emmett were going to be with Kai, and when Marco and the rest of the team got back, he was asking them to stay as well.

It had been Dinah who had given him the idea. Apparently in a traditional pack, all the closest friends of the omega were there to provide comfort during the birth. The mate, the midwife and alpha were always present as well. In this instance the mate and the midwife were the same person. Isabelle had everything covered for Dinah who had declared she wouldn't miss it for the world when Kai had shyly invited her.

He had given birth to Maddox terrified and alone. He wanted all his family here this time.

Kai smiled in satisfaction as he watched Charles and Blue disappear with their charges and winced as a much stronger pain reached around his belly. "Come on," Emmett said and along with Darriel helped him onto his feet.

The other benefit of Marco going was he hadn't seen Kai's water break forty minutes ago.

They moved steadily to their rooms and Kai was again thankful for the large space. Everyone for damn sure wouldn't fit in the clinic. He'd just decided to sit down to try and ease his back when the door slammed open and Marco—followed at a run by Ryker, Fox, Red, and Chrissy—barreled into the room. "Kai," Marco croaked out and took in everyone standing there. He glanced suspiciously at him. "What's going on? We got a message to say we had to come in here."

"All of us," added Ryker.

"Okay," Fox said slowly. "But if it's okay with you, I think I'll keep my clothes on this time."

Marco whipped his head around to stare at Fox in confusion. "What?"

Chrissy and Ryker both grinned, clearly working out what Fox meant. Fox rubbed his hands and opened them palm up, glancing at them consideringly. "I mean I'm the official baby catcher, aren't I?"

Kai chuckled, then winced. Marco shook his head ruefully realizing he'd been slow and he cupped Kai's cheek. "Are you ready to get this show on the road, then?"

Kai patiently watched Marco wash his hands and get out some equipment. Ryker and Chrissy took up guard in the corners. Dinah bustled around making sure Kai had plenty of water. Emmett was excellent at rubbing backs and Darriel took charge of wiping Kai's face and hands with a cool cloth when the labor carried on until the afternoon.

Elliot Alexander Stanza was born at four minutes past three and Fox hadn't needed to catch him, because his Daddy delivered him perfectly. He got a turn at holding him though like everyone else.

A little later, when Kai had been cleaned up and their friends had tidied up before leaving, all Daddy had to do was cuddle his mate and their new son. Kai watched sleepily as Marco gave Elliot his first bottle.

And Elliot's Daddy told him how much he was loved and what a big family he'd been born into and who his older brothers were and promised he would meet them tomorrow. Kai yawned and closed his eyes feeling Marco's gentle kiss on his forehead.

And decided that while he definitely wanted to wait a while—*a long while*—he wouldn't mind doing all this again.

It must be love.

Or insanity.

A month later to the day, Kai helped Marco chose a shirt after he had discarded three. To say his gorgeous mate was nervous was putting it mildly. Katrina was now fourteen and Zeke was flying her back to the pack house. There hadn't been any security concerns at the apartment and it had been decided she was safer there. Regina and two of the clan elders would be there to officially hear Marco back her when she declared her majority. Trina had loved being with Zeke and May, and she was grateful, but she was also ready to learn how to be a Panthera. Regina had been honored to accept the responsibility, which she could now do.

Marco would have loved to have Trina with them, but only Regina had the ability to keep her safe until she reached the all important age of twenty-one at the very least. As soon as she was declared independent from the Stanza clan the elders would inform Elena.

Kai carried Elliot outside and Marco balanced Maddox on one hip and clutched Luca's hand in his. They heard the sound of a car coming through the pack gates. Regina got out—elegant in Chanel as always and surrounded by huge panther shifters—and immediately hugged and kissed Emmett and Josie. She accepted the drawing Calvin had done for "grandma" in the same delighted manner she had accepted the name the first time he had called her that. "Grandma" apparently as she had confided to them afterwards was acceptable. However, if anyone tried to add "great" before it she would set her claw on them.

Marco glanced at Ryker. "Have you heard from Zeke? Shouldn't they be here by now?" He looked anxiously at the empty sky just as his phone rang. Ryker reached over and grabbed Maddox so he could answer it. Kai's heart picked up a sudden furious pace as he watched Marco go from alarmed to flat out panic in the space of two seconds. "Are you safe?" he practically shouted and Chrissy, Red, and Fox all immediately looked over and stopped what they were doing.

"What is it?" Ryker urged as he handed Maddox over to Dinah.

Marco pressed the speaker button and Trina's voice came through. "I'm on board, but Marco, what about Zeke?"

"It's okay Trina, just get here. Hang tight." He clicked the phone off and turned to everyone. "They were just getting in the helicopter on the roof of the apartment building. Three shifters, who Trina guesses were claw, managed to get on the roof. Zeke shot at them, but they shifted. He ran at them still shooting and ordered his driver to get Trina on board and away. The chopper will be here in a few minutes with her."

"What?" Emmett said, pushing through the crowd surrounding Marco. He'd clearly heard. "What about my dad?"

Marco swallowed. "Trina says they took him. As they were flying away, she saw the claw dragging him between them towards the stairs." Emmett sobbed out a breath and Ryker got to him quickly.

"He's not dead, Emmett. We'll find him," Ryker promised.

But would they? Marco knew this was either the Panthera's or his brother's last desperate act to get to Trina before she could be officially made independent.

Zeke had gotten in the way. And he was a human against some of the most lethal shifters in existence. He glanced at Emmett; Emmett turned to

Ryker and cried. Then Marco heard another soft sound of distress and turned seeing Darriel.

Like everyone else, he assumed because Darriel never talked about Zeke that he had gotten over whatever had briefly flared between them. But as he took in Darriel's wide-eyed, completely devastated expression he realized that they'd been wrong.

Very wrong.

And Marco had absolutely no idea what to say.

About the Author

Bullets and Babies

Victoria Sue has spent the last six years creating lots of stories, and sometimes other worlds, where boys can fall in love and lust with other boys. Not that she makes it easy for them and has often been accused of plotting many evil ways her guys have to struggle through to get their Happy Ever After.

These days, most of them have to dodge bullets, serial killers, and even kidnappers in between having contractions and concentrating on their breathing exercises.

After all, everyone knows that while making cute babies is fun, actually giving birth can sometimes be a little harder.

www.victoriasue.com

For the latest news, deals, stories and more, signup for Victoria Sue's Newsletter.

Facebook Group

Also by Victoria Sue

Love MPreg?

Check out these series and single title by Victoria Sue.

Standalone Novels

Daddy's Girl*

An Alpha who hates omegas. An omega who hates Alphas. Forced together by circumstances, both men are determined to see their arrangement through. Except the longer they stay together, neither of them is sure they want it to end.

Series

Sirius Wolves*

According to legend, when humankind is at its most desperate, the goddess Sirius will send three of the most powerful werewolf shifters ever created to save mankind. The alphas, Blaze, Conner and Darric, find their omega in Aden. They become true mates, fulfilling the ancient prophecy and forming Orion's Circle. Now, the battle against terrorist group The Winter Circle has begun.

Shifter Rescue*

9 1 1 for vulnerable shifters when there's no where else for them to run.

Unexpected Daddies

Daddy kink with heart and heat. No ABDL.

Heroes and Babies

Protective men find love while fighting to save a child. Contemporary suspense with heart-pounding action.

Guardians of Camelot

Hundreds of years ago, facing defeat, the witch Morgana sent monsters into the future to vanquish a humanity King Arthur wouldn't be able to save. The King might have won the battle, but now, centuries later, a few chosen men will have to fight the war. To battle an ancient evil, the greatest weapon each hero will have is each other.

Enhanced World

This series follows an enhanced H.E.R.O. team to provide the right mix of action and romance. This series is the perfect for fans of romance with a blend of military/law enforcement, urban fantasy and superheroes. As one reviewer put it, "This story was like S.W.A.T. meets X-men meets The Fantastic Four."

His First*

Omegaverse at it's finest! Set in the future, these novels pack in all the feels, while still wrapping up with a wonderfully sweet ending. Whether you've never tried MPREG or you're just looking for your next favorite Alpha/Omega pairing, check out the His First series.

Rainbow Key

Rainbow Key is an idyllic island retreat off the west coast of Florida. Think wedding destination, white sandy beaches, lurve... except at the moment Joshua is struggling to pay the electricity bill, they've no paying customers, and even if they did they can't afford the repairs from the devastating hurricane that struck three years ago. Then there's Matt who just got let out of prison, Charlie who ran away from home, and Ben, a famous model until a devastating house fire destroyed his face. Welcome to Rainbow Key — held together by love, family, and sticky tape.

Kingdom of Askara*

The Kingdom of Askara has been torn apart by conflict for centuries, where humans exist as subservient beings to their werewolf masters. Legend says it will only be able to heal itself when an Alpha King and a pure omega are mated and crowned together, but a pure omega hasn't been born in over a thousand years.

Innocents

A captivating historical duology set in Regency London. The Innocent Auction: It started with a plea for help and ended with forbidden love, the love between a Viscount and a stable-boy. An impossible love and a guarantee of the hangman's noose. The Innocent Betrayal: Two broken souls. One so damaged he thinks he doesn't deserve love, and one so convinced he would never find it he has stopped looking. Danger, lies, and espionage. The fate of hundreds of English soldier's lives depending on them to trust each other, to work together.

Pure

A madman has been kidnapping, torturing and murdering submissives. Join Callum, Joe and Damon as they race against the clock to stop the killings, while they each find love with a submissive. This trilogy of romantic thrillers is set against the backdrop of BDSM club Pure.

Hunter's Creek*

The Hunter's Creek novels will draw you in with action and keep you hooked until each satisfying HEA. This series won't disappoint fans of shifters, fated mates or MPREG.

*Stories contain MPREG

Made in the USA
Middletown, DE
06 August 2023

36236944R00113